I've travelled the world twice over,
Met the famous: saints and sinners,
Poets and artists, kings and queens,
Old stars and hopeful beginners,
I've been where no-one's been before,
Learned secrets from writers and cooks
All with one library ticket
To the wonderful world of books.

GRANDMA TYSON'S LEGACY

Anne Tyson's life was in turmoil, her mother widowed as a young woman had set up a small business making home-made biscuits. Now, twenty years later, it was a successful enterprise in a factory employing many people. Suddenly, her mother was planning to sell the business, leaving Anne to help run it with the new owner's manager, an attractive, debonair young man, Robert Fordham. Anne's fiance was pushing for an early marriage and a trip round the world, but Anne couldn't make up her mind.

Love is
a time of enchantment:
in it all days are fair and all fields
green. Youth is blest by it,
old age made benign: the eyes of love see
roses blooming in December,
and sunshine through rain. Verily
is the time of true-love
a time of enchantment—and
Oh! how eager is woman
to be bewitched!

1

THE day began with a telephone call from her mother. It was just after seven o'clock and Anne was barely awake. Her mother's voice came clearly and capably across the three hundred miles which separated them: "Darling, I am sorry to wake you up but I thought I must get on to you right away. I can't come back today. They've all got the 'flu now, including silly Gerda. Sarah was due to come out of hospital today but I've stopped that. I shall stay here until everyone's better. Sarah can't come to a sick household with a new baby and Bobby's useless, he's flapping about like a wet hen. Will you tell Beryl to cancel all my appointments, and also tell her I shall phone her as soon as possible. I have a lunch date with a man called Robert Fordham: tell Beryl to get hold of him and make it another time—" she hesitated briefly, as though thinking aloud, "No, I have a better idea, you take him out to lunch . . ."

"Oh, Mother—"

"You haven't got a lunch date?"

"No, but . . ."

"That's settled then. I've booked a table at Highwray Manor. Be nice to him and show him round the factory. He's an interesting man and will be useful to us . . . you'll like him . . ."

She drew breath and Anne managed to get a word in: "How is Sarah? And the baby?"

"They're fine. All's well in that direction and nothing to worry about. How's everything with you? Have you heard from Hargreaves? Did Barker get that order off to Switzerland? Did you clear up the business of their own name with the shop in Harrogate?" The questions about work came thick and fast. Anne managed to make satisfactory answers to all of them. Finally her mother turned her attention to the farm. "And the lambing?"

"We had three more last night; all okay, one set of twins."

"Good, good. I'll ring you at the office later in the day. I shall be at home if you want me for anything. Bye, darling."

The phone went dead with a decisive

click. Anne echoed the sound with a faint groan. In her mind's eye she could see her mother put the receiver down quickly and spring up to get on with the business of living. She would probably be dressed even at this early hour, and ready to go. No wonder poor old Bobby was flapping about like a wet hen. He was afraid of his mother-in-law and she was probably creating havoc in their cosy, untidy existence, trying to impose order on chaos when they much preferred chaos.

Bobby Coleman worked in TV and kept irregular hours. He had met Sarah, Anne's eldest sister when she was working as a research assistant in a TV studio in London. He and Sarah had two children and now they had just had a third. Her mother had decided she had to go down to London to take charge of the Coleman household while Sarah was in hospital. It was bad luck that the children—who should have been in school—and Gerda, the au pair, had to go down with 'flu when the new baby was due to come home.

Oh, well. Anne sighed and lay back in her pillows. No doubt Mother was coping and driving poor Bobby up the wall. Her mother had so much energy that sometimes Anne thought the little vessel which held it, her small compact body, would explode like nuclear fission.

But then, thought Anne, as she got up and began the business of dressing herself for the office, her mother had needed all her energy to face what life had offered her. Dear, loving, aggravating Mother. Where would she and Sarah and her other sister, Jenny, have been without their mother's energy? They certainly wouldn't have been able to enjoy so many of the good things; to have the luxury of choosing exactly what they wanted to do when they left school.

Sarah and Jenny might complain of their mother's overpowering personality and bossiness but she had never stopped them from doing their own thing. Yet she had hated it when Sarah had chosen to go to London to work; hated it equally when Jenny went on that trip to the US, and been hurt afterwards when Jenny had returned to England and had decided to stay in London. Her mother was a powerful lady, but she was also soft and vulnerable.

"You'll be going next," she had said to Anne after Jenny's decision. "I know my chicks have got to leave the nest but it's terrible all the same." Tears had come into her eyes and she had rubbed them away in irritation at herself.

"I shan't leave," Anne had said quietly, and she knew that she couldn't. But she also knew that for some reason she could stand up to her mother better than either of her sisters. Her mother was reasonable enough if you put your point of view reasonably. It was only when anyone stormed and ranted that she stormed and ranted back.

Yet she, too, in her way, had rebelled against her mother's domination. She had not run away from home like her two sisters. Instead she had chosen to fall in love with a man her mother could not approve of. She was not married to him yet but she was determined to marry him eventually. But, and she supposed this was where her sense of compromise came in, she wanted her mother to change her opinion, to like Jack, to appreciate his charm and worth. It was hard going, and Jack didn't always help. But at least her mother now recognised she was serious, that she was truly in love.

Anne brushed her thick brown hair back from her face. She had been told she was like her father and, judging from the snapshots of him, she probably was. Her sisters were too like her mother for them all to agree like turtle doves.

She went downstairs to get some breakfast.

The next thing that happened was a visit from Jimmy Dickson as she was eating her boiled egg. He came into the farmhouse kitchen, smelling pungently of sheep, and told her morosely that the twin lambs born the night before had both died. There was no apparent reason, they were big strong lambs, but the "yow", the mother, also looked bad now. After drinking a cup of coffee, he went off mumbling gloomily to himself about twin lamb disease. Jimmy was the shepherd who looked after her mother's flocks. He had recently got married and lived in the little cottage at the farm gate. He was the son of one of their neighbours and had ambitions to farm his own land one day but with prices of farmland being what they are, this was an ambition not easily to be realised. Of course, he would come into his father's farm one day, but as he said himself "You can wait a long time for dead men's shoes."

Her mother would be fed up about losing the twins, especially as she, Anne, had said all was well so prematurely. So far they had not had a very good lambing season.

Jimmy's wife, Maureen, arrived just as Anne was going. She came in every day to tidy up the house, with some help from Mrs. Braithwaite who drove in from Athelstone two or three times a week. Anne passed the time of day with Maureen, a bright-eyed, pretty girl who had been a hairdresser before she was married and who had plans to set up in business on her own and travel round, doing hair in customers' own homes. They discussed this project for a moment. Anne thought it a very good idea and that the farmers' wives roundabout, as well as less busy women, would be delighted to have her services. Maureen said she was going to do some cooking and would Anne like a nice hot-pot for when she came home? Anne said she would and set off on her journey of eight miles into the town of Athelstone.

Her mother's factory was on the other side of the town. It was a pretty spring day and, as always, as she drove down the curving highway, Anne's heart lifted at the views around her. This landscape was always changing. Sometimes, as today, the hills seemed made of plushy velvet; grey and green velvet. They looked as if they would be as soft as cushions to roll down. But they could be dark and mean and menacing. Or hazy and mysterious like Chinese scroll paintings. Or brilliant and diamond-etched with sunshine. They had a million faces, all of them different.

She passed through a village, built in a mixture of styles: old grey Victorian solid houses, sitting next to low-roofed, eighteenth century structures of even more solidity with three-foot walls built to withstand the siege of wind and weather, or flanked by pert and often ugly little modern bungalows. They were on all levels, clinging precariously to the stony hillside, perched above the road or down in a dip so that only the rooftops were visible. Everywhere there were daffodils and narcissi and splodges of forsythia and flowering currant.

She passed the end of the lane which led to Cragfall Farm, and on a sudden impulse turned up it. She would just go and say hello to Jack. She would be seeing him this evening for supper but so what? It would be nice to see him this morning too.

Cragfall was a mile from the main road, the lane which led to it winding up into the fells. She came to the huddle of buildings and drove into the untidy yard. Chickens squawked round her feet as she got out of the car and dogs barked inside the house, but no human being came to greet her.

The sixteenth century farmhouse was built into the side of a hill, well protected from the north-east winds. Made of stone, it had once been painted white, but that was a long time ago and it was now a mossy grey colour.

At right-angles to it was an equally ancient barn, and there were further buildings, a cart shed, shippon, pig pens, hen houses, all as mossy as the house and in as great a need of a coat of paint on doors and windows.

Cragfall had once been a hill farm with its sixty acres round the homestead, supporting a good flock of sheep, a cow for the household, pigs in the styes, with several hundreds of acres on the fell for common grazing and turbary, peat cutting.

But about ten years ago, when the old farmer whose family had been there for three generations had died, his wife had sold up; the land had gone to neighbouring farmers to make their own spreads more economic, the house and buildings with ten acres or so had gone to a young couple from London, Myra and George Bracken. They were into self-sufficiency and the good life, and proposed to grow their own food and get back to nature. They were still there, now with two small children, four and two, older and wiser, still growing their own vegetables, still pursuing the natural life.

Anne had met them at an exhibition of Myra's paintings, because of course Myra painted. George was a potter and also tried his hand at modelling in clay. He taught art twice a week at one of the local schools. They lived an entirely haphazard life, obeying no rules, as far as Anne could see, about tidiness, punctuality or routine. Often their kitchen sink was left for days full of dirty crockery. Their meals seemed to have no set times. Since the arrival of the children perhaps there had been a little more regularity in their lifestyle, but it was minimal.

Jack Cooper was a friend of theirs who had come for a weekend about six months ago. He was a journalist, it appeared, on the racing pages of a London paper and he had just given up his job because he was sick of the rat race, if not horse racing.

The first weekend Anne met him she also learnt that he had just had an enormous win on the races. He was a very volatile, lively man, full of ideas. Anne had never met anyone like him before and she fell deeply in love. Jack reciprocated her feelings. It was immediate for both of them and Jack could not drag himself away from her. The weekend stretched into a week, and then two weeks, a month.

When Myra and George had first bought Cragfall, they had had ideas of doing bed-and-breakfasts in the summer season for hikers and tourists, and they had cleaned out the top floor of the barn and fitted it out with bunk beds and simple cooking and sanitation arrangements. But, like a lot of their ideas, this one had come to nothing. The barn was empty. Why didn't Jack become its tenant? He moved into it,

11

went back to London briefly, and brought some possessions up: his typewriter, clothes, books, a hi-fi.

He was going to take a year off, and write a book with a racing theme. He would do a bit of freelancing in between to keep the pot boiling. He had masses of contacts, it wouldn't be difficult.

He asked Anne to marry him.

"What do you propose to live on?" her mother had exploded. "He hasn't even got a job! And what is more, where?"

"I thought you would like us to stay with you for a while," Anne had said tentatively.

"Is that Jack's idea? You realise Jack's only asked you to marry him because he knows you're too old-fashioned to live with him?"

"Oh, Mother!" It had been Anne's turn to explode.

It had seemed to her such a sensible solution. She could marry Jack, go on living and working with her mother. The house was big enough for them all with room to spare. She would hate to marry and leave her mother all on her own.

"Marriage is a very big step," her mother had protested "One doesn't embark on it like catching a bus or rearranging the furniture. You are being so mundane about it."

"That's why people live together, because it's a big step they don't want to take without trying it out first, and you don't like that either."

"Oh, phooey," her mother said. "Women have been conned into losing the protection marriage gives them, bleating about freedom and all that rot—what's free about being tied to a typewriter or a factory bench? No one's free in this life."

Anne was remembering the argument, and the fuss when Sarah had lived with Bobby before marrying him, as she crossed the yard and went up the outside staircase which led to Jack's quarters. She was not mundane; she was practical.

In the end they had compromised. Anne had promised to do nothing precipitately. She would wait a while until she had known Jack longer. "Until you are sure," her mother had said. "But I am sure," Anne had repeated stubbornly. "Until *I* am sure then," her mother had said gently "I would be so much happier if he had a proper job."

"He's taking time off to write a book."

"Very enterprising," her mother said. To her, Jack was the same as his friends, Myra and George Bracken, all of them drop-outs and hoboes. They had refused to come to terms with life's problems and challenges and retreated and opted out. Her dear daughter Anne deserved better.

The top floor of the barn was huge, with a high raftered ceiling. It had not been divided with proper walls, but Jack had contrived eating and sleeping areas with the aid of screens, papered and painted by Myra in the Chinese style. For heating and cooking he depended on electricity and he was standing now in the kitchen part of his domain, by the stove, in his dressing-gown, making himself some coffee; its aroma hung in the air, delicious and appetising.

"Darling," he said when he saw Anne. "What a lovely surprise!"

Jack Cooper was a man of medium height, slightly-built and of quite exceptional good looks. His eyes were deep blue and his black lashes so thick that on a woman you might be forgiven for thinking they were false. His hair was black and curly and worn fashionably long. But apart from his good looks, there was a warmth about him which invited trust and confidence. He was interested in people— even the dullest seemed to have something for him; and, in consequence, even the dullest blossomed under his intense regard. But, apart from this warmth, there was also an underlying sadness to his personality, as though life had surprised him with its harshness, a little-boy-lost quality which brought out the maternal instinct in most women. Anne indeed longed to make things come right for him.

"Have a cup of coffee?" he asked Anne now, after hugging her and giving her a loving, lingering kiss.

Anne hesitated. "I don't think I'd better," she said "I oughtn't to have come at all really. I have a full day ahead of me, with Mother still away."

"Now you're here, you're going to stay and have some coffee," he said firmly, pouring out two mugs. "Everything's all right with Sarah?"

"Everything's fine, except they've all got 'flu."

"But your mother is coping in her usual magnificent way."

Anne looked at him warily across the top

of her coffee-cup but he was not making fun; his expression was serious. Jack always praised her mother generously; sometimes too generously. He knew she did not like him but seemed determined not to let her dislike blind him to her worth or affect him in any way.

They chatted companionably for a few moments. Reluctantly she got up to go. He caught hold of her and kissed her again, long and passionately, and she felt her will-power going. She relaxed in his arms and felt his lips move over her face and neck in little butterfly kisses. "Darling," he said softly, "you're so sweet," and released her at last.

"See you tonight?" she asked a little unsteadily. "Shall I pick you up on my way home?"

"Great. I'll be ready. By the way, love, could you lend me a fiver? I'm broke and I don't want to go into town to cash a cheque, but I owe Myra a few bob for cigarettes."

Anne fished in her handbag and produced the money. "You're sure that's enough?" she asked.

"Of course. What can I spend it on? I'm going to sit at my typewriter all day."

Anne drove off to work, pushing down and refusing to admit her feeling of discomfiture.

She had lent a lot of money to Jack just lately. Some he had paid back and some he hadn't. He seemed to forget actually how much he had borrowed and she didn't like to tell him. It seemed so mean and cheese-paring somehow. His own attitude to money was that of a rich young man, carefree and careless. From what he had told her, she knew that he had saved up enough to take this year off from working, but apart from that she guessed he had other assets or he would not be so foolhardy or so brave as to gamble everything on this book he was writing.

She pushed the thought of the borrowed money away from her as she drove through the town. Jack had been incredibly generous to both her mother and herself, buying them beautiful presents from time to time: a lovely and expensive handbag for her mother, some scent for her—he had taken the trouble to find out the one she preferred—and frequent bouquets of flowers in the six months he had been at Cragfall. The presents had done little to soften her mother's view of Jack, although Anne, in any case, did not think that was his motive. He was naturally generous. "I agree he wants to please," her mother had said a little sourly when a huge azalea plant had arrived for her.

Anne was on the dual carriageway now, past the estuary, on through the winding streets of Athelstone to the other side of town.

Athelstone was an old, North Country market town with no frills, and downright, upright, solid, sober citizens who knew what was what. Its charter for a weekly market had been granted by Edward I in the thirteenth century but it wore its antiquity lightly; rather ignored it, in fact.

It had some large, detached, eighteenth century, four-square houses on the outskirts, and smaller eighteenth century and earlier terrace houses in the town. The large houses had been taken over by schools or the Ministry of Agriculture and Fisheries; the smaller terrace houses with their important porticoes and doorways were painted in such colours as purple and bright blue, picked out in viridian green for contrast, with no regard or solemn reverence for the past. Soon some worthy conservation antiquarian body would come along and tell the owners they couldn't and shouldn't do this, but for the moment the owners, bent on cheering the place up, were left to their own taste.

Athelstone had a lot of good shops, especially food shops. Small butchers, selling delicious home-killed beef and lamb, and their own recipe Cumberland sausages and black puddings. And bakers whose premises smelt always of fresh bread since the bread was baked behind the shop and was put on the shelves still warm from the oven—crusty bloomers and togies and twists and baps and barm cakes and currant pasties. There were pie shops selling the best pies in the whole world which were also baked behind the shop, and sometimes you had to be very careful when you bought them for the gravy was oozing out, hot and succulent.

There were old-fashioned grocers, with mahogany shelving topped with Chinese tea canisters, who sold raisins and rice loosely by the pound—no metric nonsense for them, and much cheaper than ready-wrapped—and spices and fresh yeast by the ounce. Athelstone was a very good shopping town although it was an activity that took a long time, because the shopkeepers were friendly and liked to pass the time of day with their customers.

Anne had wound the car window down to get the benefit of the spring sunshine and, as she neared the factory, the most delicious smell assailed her nostrils. She was not always aware of this smell, being so accustomed to it, but today, the wind being in the right direction, she noticed it particiularly, the lovely, warm, baking smell of *Grandma Tyson's Biscuits.*

She avoided a blue-and-white truck, emblazoned with the name, which came out of the factory yard far too fast, and then drove herself in and parked in her apportioned place.

She was greeted by Beryl, her mother's secretary, as soon as she set foot in the office. Beryl was thin and middle-aged, very neatly dressed, with immaculately coiffed hair and large, fashionable specs. She was very efficient.

"William says that mixing machine has

broken down again. It's ten years old, he says, and he can do nothing with it. It's the same one that broke down last week."

"Oh, lor'. Tell him I'll be right down as soon as I've seen my mail, and, Beryl, Mrs. Tyson isn't coming back today after all. She wants you to cancel all her appointments. She'll ring you later in the day. Except the lunch date," she added and sighed, "I'm taking some man out to lunch for her."

"Mrs. Hodgson's waiting in your office," Beryl said.

"What for? I thought we sorted that argument out."

Beryl shrugged. "She says she's been thinking it over and thinks it would be better if she left after all, but she wants some redundancy payment." Beryl raised her eyes to heaven. "I think her daughter is at the bottom of it."

Anne went into the small room adjoining her mother's much larger, more luxurious office. This was her little cubby-hole where she dealt with all the personnel problems in the factory.

Mrs. Hodgson, a large lady, wearing the blue checked overall all the girls wore in the bakehouse, was sitting squarely on the chair opposite her desk.

"Good morning, Mrs. Hodgson," Anne said in a gentle voice.

"If you sacked me," Mrs. Hodgson said without any greeting, "you'd have to give me redundancy payments."

"But we don't want to sack you," Anne said. "You are one of our very best workers. I've arranged to put you in a different team so that you won't have to work alongside Mrs. Hargreaves."

"She eats all the time," said Mrs. Hodgson. "Eats pounds and pounds. I never touch a single biscuit."

"I'm sure you don't. I agree that Mrs. Hargreaves is a compulsive nibbler. Some people are, you know. They can't help themselves." Anne spoke without rancour. Compulsive nibbling by her workers was a fact of life her mother had long ago inured herself to. Anne went on, "But you won't have to watch Mrs. Hargreaves eating any more. You'll be working with your daughter alongside you. I thought you'd like that."

Anne felt like a stuck record. She had

said all this the night before to Mrs. Hodgson.

"You might like working alongside your mother, Miss Anne, but my daughter doesn't."

"Who would you like to work with then?" asked Anne.

"I've decided I don't want to work at all. I'm getting on and everyone thinks it's time I stopped. Mr. Hodgson is about due for retirement soon and we thought we'd retire together."

"I see. If you want to go, you must go, Mrs. Hodgson, but we'll be very sorry to lose you."

"I want you to sack me, then I get this here redundancy payment."

"I'll have to think it over," Anne said firmly. "Possibly we could make you an ex-gratia payment on your retirement. We'll see, let me think it over—but in the meantime, why don't you go back to work and we'll have a talk about it when my mother comes back."

She ushered Mrs. Hodgson out and put on an overall preparatory to going downstairs to the bakehouse. Beryl came in with a cup of coffee. "I thought you might need this," she said. "I really don't see why we should sack her just because she wants us to."

Anne laughed. "I think we'll have to get around that. If my mother rings, tell her I would like a word with her, although I don't think I'll bother her about Mrs. Hodgson. She can wait until she gets back." She took the cup of coffee Beryl had brought and put it on her desk. Coffee would be coming out of her ears and this would not be as good as Jack's. "How long has Mrs. Hodgson been with us?" she asked.

"For ever," Beryl said. "She's one of the old originals who helped your mother when she first started."

"That's twenty years ago."

"I think she worked here before she was married—or rather at the old chapel before we came here—then she left to get married, then she came back, then she left when she had her children, then she came back when they went to school . . ."

"We can't sack her," said Anne. "I can't understand her wanting to be sacked. At one time, she wouldn't have liked the stigma, but we'll have to give her something if she wants to retire."

"A golden handshake," suggested Beryl. Miss Anne was as soft as her mother with the girls in the factory but then they did have a nice bunch.

"Yes, Grandma Tyson can't let Mrs. Hodgson down if she's given such loyal service," Anne said smiling at Beryl's little joke.

Barbara Tyson, Anne's mother, had been widowed when she was twenty-six and left with three small girls, Sarah, aged six, Anne who was four and the baby, Jenny. Anne's father, Richard, in his thirties, had just started his own engineering works after several years with one of the largest shipbuilding firms in the area.

When they were first married, he and Barbara had bought an old sheep farm in the Lakeland fells, near enough for him to commute to Hunthorpe where his job in the shipyard was. They were able to buy it cheaply because it was old, remote and derelict and the land had been badly neglected. Richard planned to run the farm as a hobby and gradually they would get the old house to rights and modernise it. It was in a beautiful position, surrounded on all sides by rolling hills and pretty views.

For the first few years, while Richard had a salary, they were able to do some of the things they wanted to do. There was a new bathroom and a new kitchen and the land was put into better heart, but there was much more they intended to do when funds became available.

All these lovely plans had come to nothing when Richard was killed in an accident in his own works.

He was heavily in debt, and when the dust had settled Barbara found herself with the farm, three small children to support and not much else. Richard's parents were dead, Barbara's were elderly with nothing much to spare although they did their best. But she had the farm and its sixty acres.

"Sell up," her London friends cried. "Buy yourself a little house somewhere in the south. Get a job!" But she didn't want to leave the little patch she and Richard had carved out for themselves. It was his country. He had been born there. He bore a name which was very old in those parts. Besides, as well as loving Richard, she loved the northern countryside and the northern folk with their quirky, perceptive, sardonic humour and their tremendous conceited belief in themselves and their way of life. She wanted to stay in the north. She would be cutting herself off from Richard completely if she left. So she stayed, despite the consternation of her friends.

Brought up in London, with occasional forays into the soft, southern countryside, she knew nothing about farming or the rough, stony land surrounding her. She began to learn. She had kind and friendly neighbours willing to help. She worked hard and she managed, but she soon began to understand that she was going to make a poor living at best.

She had been widowed a year when she looked around for something to supplement her income. Sarah was at school now and the two littlest went to playschool two or three times a week. Possibly she could have taken a job in Athelstone but the arrangement of someone to look after the children seemed too difficult to organise.

Among Richard's possessions had been an old cook book of his grandmother's. It contained, among many others written out in his Granny's spiky copperplate, a very good recipe for ginger biscuits. Barbara had first made some of these for the food stall at the fête in aid of repairs to the village church. They were very popular and it became a regular thing for her to make a batch of biscuits for any of the local functions when funds were being raised for some good cause.

She decided to make some biscuits and try to sell them in Athelstone. She made several large batches, parcelled them up in plastic wrap, tying them with blue ribbon, and took them round to her grocer's. He was sympathetic; yes, he'd be willing to try them out. They sold very quickly and the grocer asked for more. Barbara made another lot—and another, and another. She bought a commercial mixing machine to try and speed things up. She designed a blue gingham wrapper which she had specially printed at the local printers. She called her biscuits "Grandma Tyson's Ginger Biscuits".

She tried out another variety of biscuit, spiced with cinnamon this time as well as ginger. She made another of oatmeal to be spread with rum butter, since this was the land of rum butter and every home had its own special recipe. She got a couple of girls to help her bake the biscuits. But the whole operation was becoming too large for her to handle in her kitchen.

She went to the bank and met a moderately responsive and kindly bank manager and told him her plan. She wanted to get some small premises in Athelstone where the biscuits could be made on a more commercial scale, still with their home-made flavour with the best of ingredients—fresh, newly-laid eggs, butter and brown sugar. The bank manager was helpful. He gave her a loan and she acquired on lease a small, whitewashed redundant methodist chapel, and there her biscuit company was born. That was twenty years ago. Now she had much larger premises in the old market hall, abandoned when the new market hall was built. She exported all over the world, including such unlikely places as Kuwait and France. Some posh grocers in London marketed her home-made biscuits under their own name. She had a thriving and absorbing business.

The farm was now as she and Richard had planned it long ago. Completely and lovingly modernised, but with many of its old-time features fondly preserved. The shiny smooth flags of the kitchen floor, for instance, were still there, but modern fitments sat on their sealgrey smoothness. The fields around the farm had well-kept walls and fences; the fell sheep were tough and healthy. The more pampered beasts in the fields were equally cared for along with the three fell ponies which the girls had long outgrown and which where honourably retired, all nearly as old as their owners.

Anne went into the bakehouse to see William Hardcastle, the foreman, about the broken-down machines. William, like Mrs. Hodgson, had been with her mother since the early days. In those days a broken machine was a major disaster. William still thought on those lines. He did not give up lightly but even he admitted to Anne that this machine was now beyond repair. It had broken down while full of biscuit mix and the brown, delicious, gooey stuff was being carefully scooped out of the drum.

The whole operation of the biscuit-making took place in the bright airy spaces of the old-time market. The building had been stripped to its bare essentials, the walls painted white, the floors laid with steel plates for safety's sake. Dough dropping on them would stick and not slide to cause accidents.

At one end were the stores of flour and sugar and the big chutes, in between the machines for mixing and cutting out the dough, then centrally, the ovens and finally, at the other end, the girls in teams, receiving the cooked biscuits and packing them in their individual wrappers and boxes.

It was home cooking on a very big scale.

While she was talking to William about the dismantling of the broken-down machine and the arrangements for the run of biscuits that the breakdown had interrupted, one of the typists in Beryl's office came up to her and said, "Please, Miss Anne, there's a gentleman to see Mrs. Tyson."

Anne turned. "What is it, Julia? Mrs. Tyson won't be in today. Get Beryl to see him."

"Beryl's not in her office and I told him Mrs. Tyson wasn't here but he says he's got a long-standing lunch appointment with Mrs. Tyson, and he's a bit early but he thought it would give him more time to see around the factory."

"He certainly is early," Anne said in irritation. "Tell him I'll be up in a minute or two."

She turned back to William to decide how they were going to re-jig the programme.

Julia gave her the card she held in her hand. "He gave me this."

Anne looked down at the card. *Robert Fordham*, she read and then, in one corner, *Waring & Co Ltd* Waring was a household name—an enormous food combine which manufactured jams, biscuits, pies, health foods, sauces and ketchups.

She was puzzled. How on earth her mother thought such a man would be useful to them she couldn't imagine. Waring & Co were right out of their league. She went back to her office.

The man standing by the window looking out into the street, turned at her entrance. He was much younger than she had expected, in his early thirties, tall, well-built but lean, with craggy good looks, dressed in a well-cut suit. He exuded an air of health and wellbeing and self-confidence. His appearance, attractive and personable as it was, gave her a slight frisson—of she knew not what. Alarm? Fear? Afterwards, she was to think it was premonition. This man was going to change her life and, at that first meeting, she had a warning.

His grey eyes raked her from head to foot and she remembered she was still wearing the overall she had donned to go into the bakehouse.

"I'm sorry I'm so early," he said smiling, showing some nice, even white teeth. "I take it your mother has not come in yet."

"She's not coming in at all today," Anne said. "I am Anne Tyson, her daughter, and she has asked me to stand in for her."

"I have heard of you," Robert said, "and I'm very glad to meet you."

She really was as pretty as her mother had said. A tall, slim, ethereal creature, quite unlike her charming, voluble rotund robin of a mother. He had been expecting a petite dolly-bird. She should be called Undine with that beautiful waterfall of hair and huge trusting eyes. Maybe Athelstone was going to have attractions after all.

Anne quickly explained her mother's absence. ". . . so I am afraid you will have to put up with me," she ended.

"I shall be delighted to," he said gallantly.

33

"I understand you are your mother's right hand."

Anne looked at him a little uncertainly. "You really want to look over the factory?" she asked.

"One of the reasons for my visit."

Anne longed to ask him why he wanted to see over Grandma Tyson's biscuit-making operation but the opportunity to do so did not seem to present itself as she took him on a tour of the bakehouse.

It was he who asked the questions; intelligent, knowledgeable questions about output and quantities and suppliers and markets. He was interested in all her answers.

2

AFTERWARDS, with hindsight, she marvelled at her stupidity. Of course it was perfectly obvious why he asked all those questions. But, of course, even if she had had her wits about her, she would not have believed what her wits could have deduced.

When the tour was over, and they were back in her office, he said, "It's a much smaller operation than I imagined, talking to your mother, but just as interesting as she described, and of course, the whole story of her enterprise is fascinating."

"My mother is a great enthusiast," said Anne carefully. "She doesn't mean to exaggerate—"

"Oh, she didn't exaggerate," Robert Fordham said quickly "Especially about you," he added.

"Oh dear," Anne smiled a little wryly, "you must make allowances for a fond Mamma."

She glanced at her watch. "We've got a

table booked for lunch at an hotel," she said. "Not too far away but it'll take us about half-an-hour to get there—perhaps we ought to be going."

She felt shy and panic-stricken suddenly. What on earth was she going to talk about with this very suave, sophisticated man for the next hour—or two hours at the worst? Her mother should not have wished this on her.

"Where did you meet my mother?" she asked carefully as she drove along the winding road which led to Ambleside.

"My boss met her at one of those business lunches," Robert Fordham said, "and then I met her afterwards at dinner."

He smiled at the recollection. Somehow he did not think this bright, beautiful, self-assured girl would like what her mother had said to him at that dinner when they had got to the coffee and liqueur stage: "Robert, I'd like to tuck you up under my arm and take you home to meet my very pretty daughter. We could do with a man like you about the place. Don't tell me you're married?"

"No."

"No entanglements?"

"Not at the moment."

"You're perfect. When can you come and see us?" He had not expected to come quite so soon but old James seemed to have a bee in his bonnet about *Grandma Tyson's Biscuits*—or was it Barbara Tyson?—and when James had a bee in his bonnet, steps had to be taken fast to stop it buzzing.

"Do you know this part of the world?" asked Anne, still making conversation.

"Not really, although I have worked in the industrial north." He looked out of the car window with satisfaction. "What a beautiful day it is."

"Spring is one of the best times up here," Anne said stiltedly, "but I guess that's true of most places after the dark haul of winter. I remember I was in Switzerland once in the spring and that was lovely too, all the meadows covered in flowers."

At some point during the next two hours —because it *was* two hours as Anne had feared—a spark was lit. Perhaps it was on the drive there, as she lost her shyness, up and down the hills, through the pale green woodlands, with glimpses of lovely views of water; perhaps when they reached the pretty Regency house turned into a starry hotel; perhaps when they were welcomed warmly by the proprietrix; perhaps when they chose their delicious food from the buffet. At some point, Anne suddenly realised she was enjoying herself. Robert Fordham was a charming, easy person to talk to, and amusing and light-hearted. They talked of everything and nothing— his work, her work, where they liked to go for holidays, what they read, what they saw on TV—a mishmash of conversation. He also made her laugh a lot. He had a wry ironic way of describing things. She learnt that he lived in a flat in London, that he was thirty-one, and had five godchildren and had been best man three times. "It's what happens to bachelors." She registered the fact that he was a bachelor with a little surprise. He'd make someone a lovely husband, but maybe he had been working too hard to think of marriage. Or maybe he didn't believe in marriage and the piece of paper, and had a girlfriend tucked away in his flat.

"Are you married?" he asked her suddenly, as though reading her mind, and then remembering her mother's words answered his own question immediately, "No, of course you're not."

"You sound very sure—" Anne paused and added, "I'm not married exactly."

"You said that very nicely. You're spoken for? That's very devastating news. Why do all the most beautiful girls get away from me as soon as I set eyes on them? You're engaged to be married?"

"I'm not exactly engaged either," Anne said. "I've fallen in love with a man my mother doesn't like."

"But she's not going to marry him, is she?" Robert said.

"No, but I don't want to marry someone she doesn't like. My mother and I have always been great friends. Her approval is very important to me."

"What are you going to do?" asked Robert.

"I guess I'm waiting for my mother to change her mind about Jack."

"But you love him?" he asked. "Surely if you love him, you would not want to compromise, or wait for anyone's approval?"

"I don't want to hurt my mother."

"I've always heard that real love is

39

overwhelming, the world well lost for it and all that, a kind of madness . . ."

"Have you ever been in love like that?"

"No, never. I'm not sure I believe in it."

"There you are then. You don't know. Is that why you're not married?"

They looked at each other—blue eyes meeting grey ones. Anne looked away first. She had had a strange sensation, looking into his eyes—vertigo, suffocation—not enjoyable.

"I'm not married for a variety of reasons, I suppose. Basically, I'm not against it," Robert said. "No one would have me for a start. I've been very busy working. Then I've never met anyone I want to spend the rest of my life with—marriage is a life sentence, after all . . ."

"Lots of people these days don't look on it like that," said Anne. "They chop and change, get divorced . . ."

"Very messy—no, if I get married, I want to start off at least thinking it's for keeps."

"Then perhaps you're asking for the moon, too. Maybe you'll have to compromise in the end. Or maybe you don't really want to get married?"

"Oh, yes, I'd like to get married. I'd like to have a beautiful obedient companion, to comfort me and minister to all my needs, physical and mental, a best friend to admire me and soothe me . . ."

"You could have that without being married," Anne said with asperity, "And you sound very lordly and oldfashioned."

"And you don't like that?" he said, a teasing glint in his eyes. "Your feathers are all ruffled. You won't be any man's houri?"

"I'm not the houri type."

"Aren't you? But it works both ways, you know. I'm all for equality. I'd do a bit of comforting, soothing and ministering myself—and admiring too, of course. Don't you want to be told you're beautiful?"

His eyes, bright with amusement, watched the flush which rose to her cheeks.

"Oh, I suppose so, but I want more than that," Anne said, "My mother always says 'Handsome is as handsome does', and I rather agree with her."

He put out his hand and patted hers which was resting on the table. "I mustn't tease you. You're too pretty. I always tell my sister that blushing is good for the complexion. It keeps it smooth, soft and beautiful like the ads say for soap."

"I blush for nothing," said Anne. "I mean it means nothing and it's very unkind to comment on it." Her blush deepened, as she knew it would.

"Forgive me," he said solemnly. "So your ambition is to get married and raise a family . . ."

"I never said that."

"You don't want children?"

"Of course I do. My sister's children are adorable."

"My sister's children are adorable, too," he said, "So we've that in common. Tell me more about Jack. Why is he going to be the ideal husband? Give me a few hints. I might learn how to be successful with women myself."

Anne looked up to meet his quizzical gaze. "Now you're being mock-modest. I'm sure with your line in talk you're very successful indeed."

She wondered inconsequentially how many girls had languished over him. He might never have fallen in love but she would like to bet there were some love-lorn maidens strewn behind him in the past—

or maybe even in the present. She thought, "It's time we changed the subject". Their conversation was getting altogether too personal. She did not want to talk about Jack. It was questionable whether he would be an ideal husband; it was questionable as to whether such an animal existed, or if he did, whether she wanted him. She did not know what had possessed her to talk about Jack and her mother's dislike of him.

"Have you worked for James Millard very long?" she asked.

He raised his eyebrows at her sudden change of subject but followed her lead and told her something of his association with Warings, which went back nearly six years. He had joined them a couple of years after leaving university.

He had early on decided to go into commerce. "I guess I wanted to make money."

"Doesn't everyone?"

"Some more than others—there are other things in life, after all. James Millard is a great wheeler dealer. Sometimes I think we have almost too many excitements . . . that we're getting too big . . ."

Afterwards, thinking of their talk,

especially the talk about work, Anne was surprised at her own dimness. There were other remarks which had a double sense when she remembered them afterwards. He talked a lot about a new factory which Warings were opening in the near future. He asked if it was difficult to find places to live round Athelstone. He was interested in the hotel in which they were lunching. Anne thought he must be contemplating a holiday. It was, after all, a great place for holidays.

Once he remarked, "When you meet James you will understand what I mean . . ." He was talking about his boss and gardening. James it appeared was a very keen gardener.

"So's my mother."

"No wonder they got on so famously."

He had come down from London early that morning and he planned to take a late afternoon train back.

Anne drove him to Athelstone station and waited until his train came in.

"It's been lovely meeting you," he said, taking both her hands in his and looking down at her, his eyes warm with admiration. "You're all your mother said you were, and thank you for the splendid lunch. Next time I shall be the host. I'm going to look forward to working with you."

"Working with me?" Anne looked at him puzzled.

"You *are* going to stay on?" It was his turn to look puzzled. "I understood from your mother that you would be happy to keep your job and go on working with us."

"Working with you? You mean with Warings? I don't know what you are talking about."

"Well, I know we haven't exchanged contracts yet, but our decision is pretty final. James wanted me to come down today and see for myself and I shall report back nothing but good. Although I don't think James would renege on our offer whatever I said. He is pretty keen. But I just wanted to see for myself what we are actually buying. It's not exactly a pig in a poke. We have seen the balance sheets after all."

"Buying? Offer?" Anne repeated his words in uncontrolled amazement. "What are you talking about? We are not for sale."

It was Robert's turn to look surprised. He stared at her for a moment before saying, "My dear girl, you are. Your mother has more or less accepted our offer. Of course, there are lots of details to be ironed out but basically we've agreed . . ."

"I don't believe it," Anne cried. She had gone pale.

At that moment, Robert's train rumbled into the station. There was movement all round them as passengers got on and off and the train doors banged shut.

Robert looked down at her, his brows creased with a worried frown.

"I'm sorry if I've given you a shock— it's not final, of course, but naturally I thought you knew we were interested in buying. I always understood from your mother that you must be a party to the deal. You are a director of your mother's company, I believe?"

Anne nodded. She took a deep breath and regained control of herself. "Your train," she said, "You must catch your train."

Reluctantly, Robert got into a compartment. He was at a loss for words. The memory of her stricken face stayed with him all through the journey back to London.

Anne drove like a maniac back to her

46

office and the telephone. She threw her handbag on to her desk with such a crash that Beryl looked up from her typewriter in surprise.

Furiously, Anne dialled her sister's number. She heard her mother's voice and took a deep breath. "Mother, it's me— Anne. I've just had lunch with Robert Fordham—"

"I'm so glad, darling, that you've met him," her mother broke in eagerly. "Isn't he a charming man? I'm sure you two got on like a house on fire—you have such a lot in common—"

"We got on very well," Anne said evenly, "until he told me that Warings are buying the business—our business—" she paused, waiting for her mother's denial.

There was silence from the other end of the telephone; such a long silence that Anne wondered if they had been cut off. "Mother! Are you still there?"

"Yes, I'm still here," her mother said at last. "Robert Fordham had no right to tell you that. Nothing is final yet, nothing is settled."

"He seems to think it is final."

"Well, it isn't."

"But have you even contemplated selling? Why haven't you told me? It was the most awful shock—"

"Because I wanted to be absolutely sure in my own mind before I faced you with it —because I don't want to argue about it— or be persuaded—because I don't want to be precipitate—" she hesitated. She could have added, "And because I don't want you to go and rush off and marry that Jack creature," but she didn't. Instead she went on—"Oh, darling, I can't talk about it or explain on the telephone. I have made my plans about telling you—giving you my reasons properly—"

"But whatever can be your reasons?" Anne interrupted.

"I'm tired of working. It's as simple as that—and Warings have made a fantastic offer. Your job—if you still want to go on working—will be safe. We will have shares in Warings. I can't talk now, Anne, but don't get excited. Nothing, I repeat, nothing is settled yet, and, of course, you have to be consulted. Robert Fordham has jumped the gun. I thought we were going to have a nice further exploratory talk . . ."

"But why didn't you *tell* me?" Anne almost wailed.

There was silence again and then her mother said, "I'm sorry, Anne, I didn't mean you to find out like this."

"You can give up working if you want to," Anne said, "You don't have to sell up. I can carry on if you want to retire—"

"We'll talk about it when I'm home," her mother said. "It's no good like this, over the telephone."

When Anne at last hung up, she looked across at Beryl. "Did you know about this offer?" she asked abruptly.

The other woman put a hand to her hair and pushed back an imaginary straying lock.

"Well, yes, I did," she said. Anne was not surprised. Beryl did know most of her mother's secrets and plans, was more her confidante than perhaps Anne had ever been. Anne had never resented this, understanding that her mother wanted— no, needed—someone calm, practical and of her own generation as a sounding board and adviser.

"But it's not settled," Beryl went on. "It's not final. Your mother was worried as to how you were going to take it and how she was going to tell you."

"In other words, it *is* settled in her mind and she isn't going to discuss it with me. I have got to agree to her plans. I was going to be presented with a *fait accompli* and all she was worried about was how she was going to sugar the pill."

"You're being very hard. I wouldn't put it like that," Beryl said carefully. "Your mother wanted your approval. She wanted you to understand why she is doing it. It's as much for your future as for her own— and your sisters' futures. You will all be very well off."

"I can look after my own future," Anne said angrily. "I love this enterprise. It's our thing. We've made it into a wonderful business. It's homely—we know all our workers—they're like members of our family. They won't want to be part of an enormous combine, mere cogs in a machine, run from a head office in London. It's thrilling to work for a business like this when you can see the results of your efforts so closely and quickly. It's—it's—" she searched for a word—"it's intimate and cosy and rewarding. I don't want to work for a faceless conglomerate—" as she said this, the attractive face of Robert Fordham came unbidden into her mind—"I'm my own boss here—" She broke off and put her hands to her face. She felt like weeping.

3

BUT she did not weep. She got on with the rest of the afternoon's work, making decisions like a zombie, pushing to one side problems which needed thought and concentration. She was going home early.

She packed it in at half-past four, ignoring Beryl's raised eyebrows, and drove straight to Cragfall. She wanted to talk to someone sympathetic, to explode, to vent her feelings of disappointment and disillusion. She wanted Jack.

She found him companionably having tea with Myra Bracken in the farmhouse kitchen. The two children played around Myra's feet, sitting on the stone floor busy with some wooden toys. It was a cosy domestic scene.

"Would you like a cup?" Myra asked.

Anne shook her head.

"You're home early, darling," Jack said, "I didn't expect you just yet."

"I left early."

"Is anything the matter?"

"No, not really, I suppose," Anne said and then burst out unable to contain herself any longer, "Mother is selling the business!"

Jack stared at her. "You mean giving up? Whom has she sold it to?"

"Warings."

Even unworldly Myra had heard of Warings. "That can't be bad, surely?"

"How much has she sold it for?" asked Jack.

"I don't know," Anne said, "I didn't ask."

"You didn't ask!"

"You mean she's giving it up entirely?"

"And what about you? Are you out of a job?" The questions came thick and fast and Anne tried to answer them. They were all the wrong questions. Jack didn't seem to understand how she felt.

"But, darling, you'll be free, you won't have to stay here, you can travel the world."

"But I like my job here. I like this place."

"Of course you do. But your mother is bound to compensate you for all the work

53

you've done. Surely she will settle some of the proceeds on you, that's what you deserve."

"I would rather *Grandma Tyson's Biscuits* stayed a small family business."

"Today's the day of the big battalions," Jack said cheerfully. "You can't avoid progress, darling."

"But is it progress?" Myra asked earnestly. "Will the biscuits stay the same, so delicious, so home-made tasting?"

"Who cares?" Jack asked. "Obviously, they'll stay the same if Warings think they can sell more biscuits if they do. I must admit I can't understand your mother. She has always seemed such a dedicated career woman, a mini-tycoon. She must have received an offer too good to refuse."

"That's what she said," Anne said. "And she's tired of working. She also told me that nothing's final yet."

"Oh." Jack looked deflated. "Then why are you so stricken?"

"Because I know my mother and I know it's final. She's sold the whole concern without consulting anyone."

"I can understand how you feel," Myra said after a small silence. "You have been so absorbed by it. It has been your whole life."

Anne sighed. "Well, perhaps not my whole life, but I've found it fun, planning the expansion we've had lately, finding new markets . . ." Neither of them seemed to appreciate the enormity of what her mother had done, how shattering a step she had taken.

I suppose I have set my sights too low, thought Anne miserably, been cocooned in too safe and small a world. What did it matter if *Grandma Tyson's Biscuits* disappeared into the huge maw of Warings? A little family firm, employing a few hundred people—its disappearance would cause only the faintest of ripples in the world of commerce, if it caused a ripple at all.

She wanted to talk to Jack alone, to explain how she felt. The presence of Myra inhibited her. She stood up to leave.

"Do you want to come back with me now?" she asked Jack, "or should I come and pick you up later?"

"Why don't you stay and have supper with us?" asked Myra suddenly. Dimly she perceived that Anne was in some sort of incomprehensible distress.

"There's a stew in the oven waiting for us," Anne said.

"A stew won't spoil. You can eat it tomorrow," suggested Myra persuasively.

"There are the dogs—I have to . . ."

"Jimmy Dickson will see to the dogs," Jack said.

"I want to see him too. We're in the middle of lambing . . ."

In the end she compromised. She would go back home and see to the things she had to see to, and then come back for supper.

Driving back to Lowater Hall, she marvelled at her weakness in agreeing to this plan for her evening, the exact opposite of what she really wanted to do. She wanted to be alone with Jack, to sit by the fire, to talk to him and derive comfort from his love and understanding. She liked the Brackens well enough but she did not want their company tonight.

Maureen had gone back to her own cottage but Jimmy was still about; his truck was still in the yard. Anne went in search of him. She found him leaning over the door of one of the stables. In the stable itself was a ewe with two newly-born lambs. Six more lambs had been born during the day. Four of them were in the field with their mothers, healthy and strong. These two were also healthy, strong lambs. It was the mother who was causing the trouble. She was young and these were her first lambs. Unnaturally, she didn't seem to know what to make of them and backed away every time they tried to get near her. She had abandoned them in the field and Jimmy had rescued them and penned her up with them. He held her head while the lambs nuzzled her, seeking nourishment. When they found the source of delicious milk, their tails waggled in enjoyment. They were both black and exquisitely pretty. Every so often they opened their mouths to show triangular bright pink tongues and to let out a little bleat.

However many times Anne witnessed the birth of lambs in the spring, it always seemed magical. The lambs were always so angelically pretty. Most of the ewes were model mothers, cleaning their offspring thoroughly when they were born, nudging them with their noses, watching over them. Occasionally a ewe was like this one, a naughty mother as Jimmy called it. But kept penned up for a few days with her offspring, she would gradually come to terms with motherhood and them and allow them to suckle naturally.

To Jimmy all his sheep had individual characters. There were some who were always greedy, first to arrive for the nuts with which their diet was supplemented when grass was in short supply, pushing and shoving to get the most. There were others who didn't like being hustled and who would hold back, standing on the outskirts of the mob.

There were some who were loners and who sat in the fields away from the rest; others who were terrified to be separated from the flock. To Jimmy even their faces as well as their temperaments were different and he had nicknames for them. In one characteristic they were all the same. They were sheep and where one went, the rest followed—like sheep.

Despite Jimmy's affection for his ewes, and his gentleness in handling them and looking after them, he also liked eating roast lamb.

Having heard Jimmy's account of his

day, Anne went back to the house and fed the dogs who had given her the usual vociferous welcome, the lurcher, Georgie, sleek and black, and the labrador, Dan, also sleek and black, only six months old, and full of energy and love and bonhomie.

What was her mother going to do? Was she going to sell Lowater too? It was inconceivable that she should do such a thing, but this morning she would have said it was inconceivable that she should sell *Grandma Tyson's*.

Anne took her troubled thoughts up to her pretty, chintzy bedroom, washed, changed and re-made up her face. She was going to do her utmost to persuade her mother not to sell. She would offer to take more responsibility. She knew she could run things on her own. Her mother could take things easier, have longer holidays, retire altogether if that was what she wanted. Her resolve made her feel a little better and she was almost cheerful as she made her way back to Cragfall.

They were eating in the kitchen, which was a little tidier than usual, and Jack and Anne sat at the scrubbed pine table while Myra was busy at the stove, peppering and grilling some steaks. George was engaged with a salad, arranging it tastefully in a big wooden bowl and then making the dressing with great precision, adding a bit of this and that herb and seasoning as his palate indicated. Afterwards, he would take his place at the stove to make *crêpes suzette*, pouring in brandy and cointreau with gusto and setting them alight with the concentration of a French chef. They were great cooks, the Brackens, and Anne knew she would enjoy her dinner.

"Jack darling," Myra said, turning from the steaks for a moment, "fill our glasses, will you?" Jack picked up the flagon of wine standing beside the bread-board with its home-made loaves, a crusty white one as well as the wholemeal health-giving one. The white one, glazed and shiny, was scattered with sesame seeds. Irrelevantly, Anne thought how pretty they looked, like a still-life detail from a Dutch painting.

She sipped the rough red wine and said, "I'm going to try to persuade my mother not to sell." Jack put down the wine. "Isn't it rather silly to decide that before you know how much she is selling the business for?"

"Supposing it's a million pounds?" said Myra.

Anne laughed. "Well, it won't be. I am going to suggest that Mother retires and I take over completely."

"What about me?" Jack asked quietly. "Where do I fit in?"

Anne had a sudden feeling of guilt. She realised that in all her anguished plans she had given no thought to Jack except as a comfort for herself. "I suppose I'm not thinking very straight," she said slowly.

Jack put out his hand and patted hers. "No, you're not, my love. And you're being a bore about *Grandma Tyson*. Wait until your mother gets back and the dust has settled. It's not the end of the world, you know, if *Grandma Tyson* dies the death. Especially if she leaves you a nice little legacy."

"You like yours rare, don't you, Anne?" Myra asked, interrupting. "And a well-done one for George. Here we are. I think we're ready to roll."

She put down their sizzling steaks in front of them, brought out some baked potatoes from the oven, and sat down herself to eat.

"Do you see yourself living here for ever

and ever?" asked Jack as he helped himself to salad.

"I haven't seen myself doing anything in particular for ever and ever," Anne said. "I just thought I would go on with the business, making it more successful."

"Surely your mother has really achieved success by being taken over by Warings?" asked Jack. "That's the ultimate accolade. Where can you go from there? How can you top that?"

"But I don't want to be a big business— I just like our little business."

"You'll have to get Anne to give you a job, Jack," Myra said. "That would do you good—rolling dough or perhaps you could be a salesman taking the biscuits round to the grocers. You could wear a nice blue uniform." She allowed her fancy to embroider a little and then finished briskly, "Now leave the girl alone, Jack. She's had a shock and she has to get used to it. I can't think of anything nicer myself than living here for ever and ever."

"You like living in a rut," said Jack equably, "Besides, you and George are settled with your family."

There was silence for a second or two and

then Myra, as though following a train of thought, asked casually, "How is Karen?" Jack flashed a sharp look at her but Myra was serenely cutting into her steak.

He answered, equally casually, "She's fine."

"And who is Karen?" asked Anne.

After a small pause, Jack said, "She's my daughter."

For the second time that day, Anne felt as if someone had punched her in the heart. "I never knew—" she began and could not go on. Fleetingly, she remembered Robert Fordham and their lunch-time talk about children and raising a family and their "adorable" nephews and nieces. Jack already had a family—well, a child.

"You ought to bring her up here," Myra said, as though unaware of any bombshell which had been dropped. "She'd love it."

"I might, later on," Jack said. He was staring at Anne, his expression both rueful and sad.

Anne wanted to go home but instead she finished her steak, sat on at the table while George did his *flambé* act with the *crêpes suzette*.

As soon as she was able, she made her

excuses and explained that she felt very tired and must have an early night. Myra was sympathetic. "Of course. You've had a ghastly day."

Jack followed her out. "I've got to talk to you, darling Anne." He put his arms around her and almost lifted her across the yard to the staircase leading to his quarters.

"Please, Jack, I must go home. I'm whacked."

"I've got to talk to you. I've got to explain."

She stood helplessly in the middle of the room while he switched on the lights.

"Do you want a drink?"

She shook her head. "I'm up to here with wine."

He sat on the sofa and pulled her down beside him. "Darling Anne, I didn't tell you I'd been married because it seemed irrelevant to us."

"But a child? Where is she?"

"She's with her mother. I see a lot of her when I'm in London."

"How old is she?"

"Six."

"You haven't seen much of her these past few months."

"No. I couldn't in any case. They've been abroad." Jack was silent for a moment and then he said, "I was very young when I was married, twenty-one and Karen's mother was nineteen. We didn't know what we were doing. It was hopeless, a disastrous mistake from the start."

"But why didn't you tell me?"

"I thought it might spoil things between us."

"But I would have to know eventually."

"Of course, I would have told you eventually—when I was sure of you." He kissed her gently and stroked the hair back from her face. "Darling Anne, why don't we get married? What are we waiting for?"

Anne was silent.

"It's your mother, isn't it?" Jack persisted. "I know she does not like me. She was another reason why I did not tell you about Karen. It would only have prejudiced her more than ever against me. But it's not her life, it's yours—and I want to marry you, not her. Look what she has done to you now. Has she really thought of your feelings now when she wants to sell her business?"

"I don't think she realises how much it

means to me. Besides, she has ensured my job. I can go on working for Warings if I want to."

"But do you want to? Why don't you give it all up, take your hand-out and marry me? We can start a family. We can live round here if you want to, although I think there are more comfortable places. It's pretty bleak in the winter."

"But what about *your* job, *your* work?"

"I can write anywhere. That is one of the advantages of being a journalist." He laughed. "I'll even come and work in the bakehouse if that's what you want me to do."

"Don't be silly. You have to do your own work."

He kissed her again, more passionately and Anne felt her will-power melting away. She did not like the power he had over her. One part of her wanted to give in to him, to respond to his urgency and let him do whatever he desired with such passion. Another part of her fought with these feelings. Some instinct of self preservation told her that way lay danger and disillusion.

She drew away from him. "What would you do if I said I would marry you?"

"I'd be over the moon."

"I mean practically. Where would we live for a start?"

Jack sighed. "We've been over all this before, darling. I could move into Lowater. You could come and live here. Surely it depends on what your mother is going to do? If you give up your job, we could move back to London."

"And live where?"

"I have a flat—it's rented now but I could clear them out, I suppose."

"I'd be lost in London," Anne said. "I've never lived there. But what about your other commitments? What about Karen?"

"Karen has lived all her life with her mother. There is no need to disturb that arrangement. It would be nice if she could come and stay with us sometimes. She's a darling little girl. I know you'll love her. But don't let me be so mundane, Anne darling. You'll be telling me next you want a dozen of everything, sheets, pillow-cases and stainless steel knives."

"My sister had a very big formal wedding. She wanted it and my mother certainly did."

"Very well. We'll have a big formal wedding if that's what you want." He pressed his mouth on hers again but Anne averted her face. She felt sick at heart suddenly, and exhausted. It had been a dreadful day. She rose to her feet. "I must go, Jack."

"I'll see you tomorrow?"

"I'll phone you in the morning."

He let her go reluctantly but he sensed that her moment of surrender had passed. She was her own woman again. He moved his hands down her body and round her waist and squeezed gently. "I long for you," he whispered, giving her a last, soft kiss.

A bright moon was shining in a starry sky. It was midnight and crisp and cold. The road was empty as she drove home, her head in a turmoil. She had read somewhere that every human being disappointed another human being at some time. She had been disappointed by Jack today—and her mother. Such disparate people. Perhaps she was to blame, expecting too much understanding. She was disappointing Jack no doubt. Maybe in the past she had disappointed her mother without knowing.

Lowater was ablaze with lights as she went up the driveway. What had happened? Who was there? She saw her mother's car parked in the yard. Her panic subsided but her surprise increased.

The front door opened wide and her mother's figure was silhouetted in the light streaming from behind.

Hugs, kisses and exclamations over, her mother explained, "I had to come home after what had happened. Gerda didn't have the 'flu after all. She was just exhausted, and then that nice actress friend of Sarah's, Patty Jennings—when she heard I wanted to come home—said she'd move in until Sarah gets back. She's not working at the moment so that was all right. She's very capable and efficient and everything was in good order when I left. I drove up in four and a half hours flat. It's the best time of day to drive."

"You must have exceeded the speed limit."

"Never! Oh, it's so lovely to see you, darling girl. I have been beside myself with worry over everything. What did you think of Robert Fordham? Didn't you think he was charming?"

"Not specially."

"Oh, I was so hoping you two would get along. You'll be working with him if you decide to stay on."

"I haven't decided anything—because I'm hoping to make you change your mind. Or is your mind irrevocably made up?"

"Of course not," her mother answered quickly. "I told you I thought Robert Fordham and I were going to have more discussions. I thought in any case he was having lunch again with me next week—and then you would have been able to come along and meet him properly and hear what Warings are offering exactly."

"I did meet him properly and as far as he was concerned, it was all cut and dried. I didn't realise at the time why he was asking so many questions. He must have thought me an awful idiot—"

"I'm sure he thought no such thing. He's an extremely able, charming person. The sort of man—" Barbara Tyson hesitated and did not go on.

"The sort of man?" Anne repeated.

"The sort of man I hope you'll marry," her mother finished in a defiant rush.

"Oh, Mother!" Anne, tired and irritated, flopped into a chair. "He's the sort of man

I'd never choose to marry. Far too smooth and charming and suave and all those things. And I'm the last sort of girl such a man would be interested in—a country—no—a provincial bumpkin like me."

"Really, Anne—" her mother began.

"Mother, darling, I do not want to talk about Robert Fordham and his charm. In fact I don't want to talk about anything. I want to go to bed."

"Yes, darling," her mother said meekly. "We'll talk in the morning."

4

IN the morning, after a good night's sleep, Anne felt better. She and her mother breakfasted early as was their custom. It was a beautiful sunny morning and the sun poured in the dining-room window, shining on the mahogany table, set with its pretty china and silver.

"Now, Ma, you've got to tell me everything from the beginning," Anne said cheerfully. "When you first thought of this horrid idea of selling *Grandma Tyson*, when you met this Warings man . . ."

"I would never have thought of selling *Grandma Tyson* by myself—" Barbara Tyson began. "It would never have occurred to me, but the idea was put into my head by James Millard. He's the chairman of Warings and I met him a couple of months ago at that grocers' dinner I went to in London. He became interested because Warings are opening a large factory outside Hunthorpe."

Hunthorpe was the shipbuilding and

once-prosperous industrial town a few miles further up the coast. New factories were always welcome in Hunthorpe to soak up the perennial unemployment.

"James said it would all tie up. *Grandma Tyson* will go on exactly as before but under the umbrella of Warings. It will mean more efficient distribution and marketing and so on."

"I think we're pretty efficient as we are," said Anne, noticing the 'James '. "What is this man Millard like?"

"Very nice, very sympathetic and very business-like," her mother said. "I said 'no' unequivocably at first, of course. I mean, I thought the idea preposterous and said so. I didn't want to sell. It had never occurred to me. I wondered what on earth I would do with myself without *Grandma Tyson* to worry about. But James was persistent and he told me what he would give me for the business."

Of course, Anne reflected, her mother had been bobbing about back and forth to London quite frequently lately. It hadn't all been Sarah and the babies. This James man had evidently been around.

"Tell me what James Millard offered," she said quietly.

Barbara told her and the sum made Anne take an involuntary breath.

"Yes," Barbara looked up from her plate "you may well gasp. It made me gasp. It won't all be in cash, of course. Some will be and the rest will be in shares in Warings which we will get in exchange for our shares in *Grandma Tyson*." *Grandma Tyson* was a private company, unquoted on the Stock Exchange, in which shares were divided equally between Barbara and her daughters.

"I shall settle so much on each of you—" Barbara went on. She paused a moment. "But I jump ahead. I was astonished of course, at James's offer but afterwards, when we went through the books together, I could see that it really was not so out-of-the-way, but a fair price. We are a prosperous business. We have a goodish amount of capital tied up in investment. We own the freehold of the factory site. We have ploughed all our profits back for years and years. There's plenty of room for expansion. I began to think about my own life and I suddenly realised how tired I was, how tired of my routine. I was like some rat in a cage. It had been offered escape and at first it was as though I couldn't understand what escape was—as though I was afraid of getting out of my cage . . . Am I making sense to you?"

"Yes," said Anne gently. "But you don't have to work so hard, Mother. I could take over now. You could retire."

"And take a pension?" her mother laughed. "But it wouldn't match what Warings are offering, Anne. With all that money, I will really be free."

"And what will you do?"

"I don't know yet. First I want to sort out what you are going to do. Warings want to keep you on. I stipulated that. But, of course, with your own share of the proceeds, you too might want to do something different, stretch your wings, travel, see a little of the world . . ."

"I don't think I'll want to stay on," said Anne. "I don't think I'll be able to bear to have someone else come in and tell me what to do."

"But I don't think that will happen," her mother said quickly. You will be boss of *Grandma Tyson*. Robert Fordham will be in charge of the new factory at Hunthorpe, of course, at least in the beginning and you will be under his wing, but I think you will be left very much to manage things on your own—as, after all, you have been doing for the past few years."

"And you will be seeing Robert Fordham every day," Barbara Tyson thought with satisfaction. There was nothing like propinquity for making people fall in love with each other.

Anne poured herself another cup of coffee. She had given up all ideas of hoping to change her mother's mind. Was it because the amount of money was so huge?

As though echoing her thoughts, her mother said, "You mustn't think I've suddenly gone mad about money. It's rather as if I'd been pulled up short and made to take stock of my life. In the beginning, I had to work in order to survive, to bring you up, educate you, but we've gone a long way past that now. Work has become the be-all and end-all of existence. There is more to life than work, work, work, as James says."

"But he must work very hard, surely, if he's boss of such an enormous combine?"

"Oh, yes, he does but he plays hard too. Which reminds me, Anne. He wants us to go and spend a weekend with him in the country. He has a house about forty miles outside London and he wants to meet you, and thought it would be pleasant if we both went and stayed with him the weekend after next. Are you doing anything? Is that convenient for you?"

"I think so. I'll check my diary. Have you been to his house?"

"No, I've only seen him in London, business lunches and so on. He lives in London most of the week. You'll like him, Anne, I'm quite sure."

"And if he doesn't like me, I don't get the job at *Grandma Tyson's*. I feel I'm being put on display."

"There's nothing of that about it at all. The job is yours if you want it. I would like you to stay. I would like a Tyson still to have a stake in *Grandma Tyson's Biscuits.*"

"You have some sentimental feeling left, then, for *Grandma Tyson?*"

"Oh Anne, don't be so tiresome, of course I have. But you know in the beginning it was a tough, uphill struggle. Only in the last few years has it been plain-sailing. *Grandma Tyson* hasn't been a benevolent old lady to me, rather a dragon to be conquered." She rose from the table. "It's time we went to work. You do understand I'm only doing this for the best, Anne darling? Best for me, but really best for all of us. I shall be able to give you all a little security. That is surely accomplishing something. Jenny might not care but I am sure Sarah, with her children to think about, will appreciate some security."

"We will all appreciate it, Mother. You have accomplished a lot." Anne gave her mother a quick hug. How easy it was to see her mother's point of view. "I think I'll take my car as I want to visit Jack on the way home."

"How is Jack?" her mother asked perfunctorily.

"He's fine. I had dinner with him last night."

"And how is his book coming along?"

"Fine, he's working hard." Which was not strictly true, of course. Jack hadn't spent much time at his typewriter lately. He'd been fishing with George, but there was no need to tell her mother that.

He was fishing with George when she

called at Cragfall on her way home that evening.

"Again!" Anne raised her eyes to heaven in a mock long-suffering way.

"Well, you know how mad they both are on it, and Jack nearly caught something yesterday—and of course it was huge, like all the ones which get away."

"Have they gone below the bridge?"

"They didn't say where they were going."

Anne got back into her car. "I'll go and look for them."

She drove back the way she had come, through the village and across a little hump-backed bridge, and parked the car in an out-of-the-way spot. She walked back across the bridge and stood looking at the river. It was wide and shallow at this point, the water bubbling over many flat rocks. She climbed down on to its bank. George had managed to rent some fishing for the season and had generously allowed Jack to share his rod.

She walked along the bank further away from the road. Trees bordered the path and the river here deepened into pools. It was a beautiful still evening, ideal for fishing, although the midges would be bothersome. She came across George first, standing in his waders at the edge of the water, busily casting.

"Jack's further up, round the bend," he said.

"Have you caught anything?"

He nodded his head over his shoulder and she looked down at his gear on the bank. Nestling in the grass were two glittering brown trout.

"Delicious for breakfast," George said with satisfaction.

Anne agreed with him. Delicious for breakfast, yes, but she always felt sad at the sight of the little fish, so pretty, so sparkling, such a short while before so sveltely swimming.

Jack was some yards further on, even further into the river than George. Here the water was several feet deep. He too had caught some fish, three to be exact, and like George's they were nestling in grass on the bank beside the rest of his fishing paraphernalia—the box of flies, the other rods and line and reel, the jersey he had discarded.

He looked across at her and smiled but

she sensed his preoccupation and sat patiently down on the bank beside his possessions. It was beautifully tranquil and she let the peace of the evening seep into her. During the day she had made her mind up about Jack—she was going to marry him. She was longing to tell him, to see his expression of joy and pleasure. It was one decision made. There would be others crowding in: when to get married, where and how? She did not want a great big wedding like Sarah's but her mother might. Where to live? Here, or should she go south with Jack and try a whole new environment? She had not known that he had a flat in London. Or had she? Perhaps he had mentioned it before without her taking it in. It had been a blow to her to learn he had been married before, but she understood why he had not told her. There had always been something sad about him, a hidden sadness, because the surface Jack was always ready to laugh and make a joke.

She watched him now as he reeled in his line and then waded towards the bank.

"Do you want to go?" he asked as he splashed out of the water.

"I'm quite happy sitting here," she said

lazily, "if you want to go on fishing. The midges aren't as bad as I thought they would be."

"I've caught three trout," Jack said proudly, "You can have them for your breakfast." He was like a little boy, she thought fondly. "But I ought to have caught more. There are plenty about and I thought George was told the fishing had been rather poor lately."

"That was last season—but maybe it's improving. Jack—" she hesitated, suddenly shy. He turned to look at her questioningly.

"Jack—"

"Darling, what is it? You look so worried . . ." He put his hand on her arm.

"Jack, I'll—I'll marry you—I mean, I want to set the date."

He looked at her in silence for a moment, gave an enormous whoop, and fell on her and rolled her over in the grass.

Laughing, she disentangled herself from his boisterous embrace.

"When did you come to this marvellous decision?"

"Today. Mother is definitely selling the

business and I decided I wanted a whole new life too."

"You're giving up your job?"

"I may or I may not. It depends. Anyway, I can decide that later."

"And what is your mother selling the business for? I mean how much money?"

"Oh, an enormous sum—" She told him and he whistled.

"I can go on working if I want to. Mother says she's stipulated I should keep my job, but we'll see. It depends on what you want to do, Jack, live up here, go back to London . . ."

"We've plenty of time to decide, haven't we sweetheart? For the moment, it's enough for me that you want to marry me."

"Oh, there's lots of things to be settled," Anne said happily, "but I feel so content, so restful somehow, that at least I've settled one thing. I'm going to get married."

Jack began stowing away his fishing gear, unhooking the delicate little fly from the end of his line and putting it away with a variety of other flies in a special metal box. The flies were set out between pages of plastic envelopes and he flicked them over lovingly. Watching him, as she had watched him before, Anne reflected that half of the fun of fishing seemed to be in this contemplation of all the gear you had to have—the different rods and equipment, the different lures and flies.

"What shall we do to celebrate?" asked Jack. "Let's go and crack a bottle of champagne somewhere."

"I want to go home first and tell my mother," Anne said.

"Why don't you do that and I will go back to Cragfall and clean myself up and come and collect you, and we'll go somewhere to celebrate. I'll book a table at Lakeside Manor or Dragley Farm . . ."

"They're always so full . . ." said Anne doubtfully.

"Don't worry. I'll find a place for us somewhere," said Jack. "We've got to celebrate. I'll pick you up about half-past seven."

Driving home, Anne suddenly realised she was nervous and that was absurd. But she knew her mother did not like Jack. She would not be pleased—and yet if only she would take the trouble to get to know Jack a little bit better, Anne knew she would change her mind. She was too suspicious of his very obvious charm and good looks.

Her mother was not in the house but walking round the fields with Jimmy, Maureen told her, looking at the sheep, hearing about everything which had happened on the farm while she had been away.

Anne went upstairs to her room and had a bath and changed. She picked one of her prettiest outfits to wear on this auspicious occasion, a dark blue silk suit with red silk blouse. She would need a coat as the evening might turn chilly, and she took her cream-coloured camel coat. With it over her arm, she went downstairs.

Her mother was in the sitting-room having a glass of sherry. She looked her daughter up and down. "You look very pretty," she said, "Going somewhere special?"

Anne took a deep breath and grasped the nettle, "I am going out with Jack," she said, and paused a moment, "We're going out to celebrate our engagement."

Her mother stared at her for a long moment, her mouth a little open. Very carefully she put down her sherry glass.

"You're what?" she asked quietly.

"We're going to have a celebration

dinner at Lakeside Manor," Anne repeated. "I've agreed to marry him."

"And when did you decide this?"

"This evening." Anne wished her mother did not look so furious—and, yes, appalled. "At least—I've been thinking about it for a long time, you know I have, and today I decided there was no point in shilly-shallying any more."

"You are doing this because I have decided to sell the business," her mother said. "You are doing it to pay me back."

"Oh, Mother, how can you say that? I'm in love with Jack—you know I have been for ages. You just won't accept it. You don't like him—you've a silly prejudice against him . . ."

"He's not right for you," her mother interrupted. "I know he's not right for you. You promised me you'd wait a while."

"Well, I have waited. You are changing your life—I am going to change mine."

"So this means you're going to give up your job entirely—" Barbara leapt up from the sofa where she had been sitting and began pacing about the room like a caged prisoner.

"I haven't made my mind up about that

but, in any case, I don't think you can complain, Mother dear. Please be reasonable . . ."

"I am being reasonable," her mother cried and went on incoherently, "It is you who are being utterly stupid and unreasonable. All right, I have sold *Grandma Tyson's* without telling you—it was hurtful of me. I didn't mean the news to reach you as it did—I had to clarify my own thoughts—I wanted to discuss it with you . . . I didn't want you to rush into the arms of the first man who's asked you to marry him . . . I suppose you told him how much I am getting for the business and that made you more desirable than ever . . . He's a fortune hunter . . ." Her tirade became more and more furious.

"You misunderstand Jack completely," Anne said wearily, "He's not interested in possessions or money he's happy-go-lucky —he takes life as it comes . . ."

"He's not going to be happy-go-lucky, to take life as it comes, on *my* money," her mother said angrily. "You're doing this to spite me, Anne, because I've hurt you and you know this is the way you can hurt me in return . . ."

"It's not that at all," Anne cried, stung. "I accept that you had to do what you've done . . . but I want a new life too . . ."

"But not with that—that lightweight . . ." her mother's anguish and anger seemed to increase. "Why must we have such an upheaval altogether?"

Anne began to be afraid that Jack would arrive and find them quarrelling.

"Please, Mother, please, please be reasonable . . ." How often Anne had heard her sisters urge her mother to be reasonable. Hitherto, the peppery temper and high-handedness had been reserved for them. Maybe she had always been too meek, too much her mother's shadow. Now she was trying to assert herself, almost for the first time, and her mother did not like it.

Very angry herself at last, Anne cried, "I am marrying Jack, not you! It's *my* life."

"It's your life," Barbara Tyson retorted, "and you're not going to ruin it if I can help it. I shall do all in my power to prevent you from marrying that man. He is not worthy of you."

Anne's anger evaporated as quickly as it had arisen. "Oh, Mother," she said wearily, "please don't let us quarrel like this and say things which we'll regret later. You have an exaggerated idea of my worth. I am very ordinary really and Jack is an ordinary man and we want to be happy together."

She heard the sound of a car in the driveway. "There is Jack now. Shall I ask him in for a drink? Or shall I go outside and take him away and tell him you don't wish us good fortune?"

Barbara Tyson flung herself back on to the sofa by the fireplace, "Oh, bring him in," she said coldly, "and I will drink to your health and happiness out loud—but in my head it will not be as man and wife but as separate people."

"Oh, Mother!" said Anne for the umpteenth time, and smiled exasperatedly. She went to the front door which was, as always, on the latch. "Do come in, Jack darling. Mother is waiting to drink our health."

Despite the bad beginning, the evening was, in the end, a success.

There were several good restaurants in the area and many of them were featured in good food guides. With nearly all of them, and certainly with the best, at the beginning of the tourist season, you had to make reservations long in advance. It was typical of Jack, Anne thought, that he had managed to get them a table at one of the most pleasant, in an old manor house, serving very good food, overlooking the water.

"How did you do it at such short notice?" she marvelled.

"Oh, I told them a tale," Jack said airily.

They sat first in the bar and had a drink, and Anne began to calm down.

"Your mother was very charming," Jack said. "I think she's pleased we're getting married."

"Yes," said Anne, thinking of her mother's skill as an actress. After the vile argument they had had, her mother had been sweetness itself to Jack, raising her glass to him and the future, asking friendly questions, hiding her true feelings with great aplomb.

Responding to her apparent warmth, Jack had been at his best, telling a joke or two, being amusing and gallant. Anne hoped that her mother might from now on begin to change her opinion about him.

He was in good form this evening, zany as only he could be, making her laugh; attentive and loving as only he could be, so that she felt loved and desirable. At the end of her meal, she felt on top of the world, capable of coping splendidly with her mother, her job and her new life with Jack.

They discussed their new life together in detail but not very practically.

"I fancy the South of France," said Jack, "sitting in some small, intimate bistro, drinking absinthe . . . Or the South Seas, reclining on a silver-white beach, drinking fresh lime juice through a straw."

"I've always wanted to go to China," said Anne wistfully.

"Why don't we? And South America? We could write a travel book together . . . Why do you want to go to China? It's not all Ming china and embroidered Mandarin robes, you know . . ."

"We could live in London," Anne said, and Jack pulled a face.

"Now you're being prosaic. Let your imagination run away with you. The world is our oyster . . . I feel I could push it off its axis . . . let's do it together . . ."

"I want to share everything together,"

Anne said, "That's what marriage means to me, I guess, sharing . . ."

Jack blew her a kiss, "You're very serious, darling—that's why I love you. Sometimes I'm not serious enough, so people tell me. You'll be very good for me. And I shall be very good for you—take your nose away from the grindstone sometimes . . ."

It was just as typical of him as securing the table that, at the end of their succulent meal, he didn't have enough money to pay for it. And neither did he have his cheque-book or his credit card with him.

"You're hopeless," Anne said laughing. Fortunately, she had enough money on her as well as her cheque-book. As she handed over the notes, she heard her mother's voice saying, "He's not going to be happy-go-lucky on *my* money," but she shut her ears to it. What was money after all? Jack was careless about it. She would just have to be careful for them both.

Her mother was still up when Anne arrived home. Suddenly tiredness had hit her and after the excitements of the day she longed for her bed. Her mother, as always, wanted to talk.

"Robert Fordham phoned while you were out," Barbara Tyson said. "He's driving up tomorrow morning early and I suggested he could spend the night here instead of staying in a hotel. Would you stay home and greet him? I have got to be in my office early tomorrow. I've got those French people coming."

"What time is he arriving?"

"He's leaving London about seven, so he should be here around noon."

"Surely I don't have to stay here all morning just to meet Robert Fordham? Maureen can show him his room and all that. Is he coming to the factory?"

"Oh, this visit is nothing to do with us," her mother said quickly. "I'm sure I told you Warings have bought a big site just out of Hunthorpe where they are going to build a big factory and redevelop the old one. That's Robert's pigeon. He's going to be in charge of the whole new operation."

"And *Grandma Tyson* is going to be a mere unimportant detail in the overall enterprise?"

"Now, Anne, don't be nasty. *Grandma Tyson* just fits in neatly with their arrangements. How was your evening?"

Anne yawned. "Lovely. We had a super meal and made lots of plans." She looked at her mother and smiled fondly, "Life seems to have turned upside down, doesn't it? It's all rather exciting. I must go to bed now or I'll fall asleep on my feet. I'll stay in and wait for Robert Fordham. I'd quite like a lie-in, although it will feel very wicked on a weekday."

"What sort of plans were you making?" her mother asked, "Let's take one thing at a time, Anne darling. I can't make arrangements for a wedding while all this business of the sale of *Grandma Tyson* hangs over us."

"I'm not asking you to make arrangements for a wedding," Anne said, "I just wish we could slip away and get married quietly without any fuss." At her mother's look of alarm, she added, "Don't worry I won't do that, but it would be nice if we could."

In the morning, she had her lie-in as she had promised herself and a leisurely bath. She was only just dressed and ready when she heard the crunch of wheels on the gravel drive. She looked out of the window and saw Robert Fordham get out of a long, sleek car. Either he had left London earlier than planned or he'd been driving too fast. Watching him walk towards the house in long easy strides, she thought he was better looking than she had remembered. She could quite see why her mother liked him so much. He was very personable. She remembered the last time she had seen him at the railway station, staring after him, as the train moved out, with that dreadful shocked feeling in possession of her heart. He must have thought of her as a fool. However much her mother had praised her work, nothing could obliterate the fact that her mother had not confided in her the momentous news of the impending sale. She had been cut down to size. Robert Fordham was not likely to pay much attention to her opinions. She was not as important as she had always thought she was in *Grandma Tyson's Biscuit Co*. She had a slight feeling of trepidation as she went downstairs to meet him.

5

ROBERT FORDHAM greeted her warmly "Hello, how nice to see you again! How are you? I wasn't sure there would be anyone about. Your mother said she had to be in her office."

Nervousness made her abrupt. "I'm fine thank you. Do bring your case in and I'll show you to your room."

He exclaimed at the prettiness of the house as he came in as most people did, bending his head to avoid the low lintel, staring round as she took him up the crooked stairway to the landing with its uneven floor which led to the bedrooms. She showed him the bedroom he had been allocated and the adjoining bathroom and waited downstairs.

He joined her in the sitting-room a few minutes later, looking appreciatively round and then out of the window at the beautiful view of hills and fields and sky. "What a pretty place! No wonder you love it so much."

She offered him a drink but he refused it. "I'm going to dash off," he said. "It's very rude of me but I've got an appointment with my site manager and I'll be spending the afternoon with him."

He turned away from the window and looked at her directly "I'm sorry I left you with such surprising news the last time we met," he said. "I got a real telling off from James for jumping the gun but I thought it was all over bar the shouting—a settled thing. I didn't realise any more discussion had to take place."

"That's all right," Anne said stiltedly. "I don't think any more discussion has to take place."

"You've agreed with your mother then —to sell?"

"Oh yes, of course." She was not going to admit any doubts to this man. He was the enemy as far as she was concerned.

She had told him so much about herself during the lunch they had had together. Now she bitterly regretted her confidences and could not understand what had come over her. He was too persuasive and sympathetic.

He smiled. "That makes me feel much

better. Now I am afraid I must be off. I'll see you this evening?"

"I expect so."

Having seen him on his way, Anne went to the factory. During the afternoon, to her surprise, Jack turned up with a ring. It was a pretty Victorian thing of silver: two little silver hands clasping a blue zircon.

"Do you like it?" he asked "The man in the shop said he'd change it if you didn't."

"I love it," said Anne warmly and let him slip it on her finger. He held her to him for a few seconds. Anne drew away first. "Beryl will come in."

"I can kiss my fiancée if I want to," Jack said "There's nothing wrong in that, is there?" He pulled her towards him again and kissed her firmly on the mouth and then let her go.

Anne did love the ring but somehow she did not feel happy. She did not know what was the matter with her. Surely this should be one of the most joyous times of her life, engaged to marry the man she loved, happily planning their future together? Her contentment of the day before had evaporated. She felt harassed, almost she might say alarmed, at the thought of their future together, despite what she had said to her mother last night. Life had been turned upside down, though it wasn't exciting but troubling. Was it all because of her mother's disapprobation? But she *had* to be independent—she must learn to be.

"Come and have dinner with us tonight," she said to Jack. "You'll be able to meet one of the big white chiefs of Warings. He's staying with us overnight."

Jack went away and Anne showed the ring to Beryl and her mother.

Her mother put on her spectacles the better to examine it. "Very pretty," she said at last.

"Very unusual," said Beryl.

"I have asked Jack to dinner."

Her mother did not look too pleased. "Oh, good," she said. "Did you see Robert Fordham? You know he'll be in for dinner? Will there be enough?"

Anne and her mother shared the catering of the household and this week it had been Anne's turn to buy the food and plan the meals. "Of course there will."

"That's all right then. Do you think we

should ask anyone else to make it more amusing for Robert?"

Mother and daughter stared at each other. "Why make it more amusing for Robert?" Anne thought, "Why not make it more amusing for Jack?" She said nothing but shrugged.

"Robert might want to talk business," her mother said thoughtfully. "I won't ask anyone else."

Anne went upstairs to tidy herself up as soon as she got home. Her new ring which she was wearing winked at her when it caught the light as she changed her clothes. Was she really going to get married to Jack? Why didn't she feel ecstatic, then, as though she could climb mountains, push a house down? Why did she feel so agitated and nervous?

Both Jack and Robert had arrived by the time she got downstairs again. She had changed into slacks and a bright shirt. Her mother had lit the fire to take the chill off the spring evening and the air was permeated with the pleasant scent of wood-smoke.

Both men turned to greet her as she walked into the room. She was accustomed to Jack's look of admiration but she could swear that Robert's eyes lit up as readily at the sight of her, as though he found her delectable.

Jack was looking tidier than usual. His hair was slicked back and he had changed into black cords and a spotless white shirt. She was pleased with him. He looked poetic and interesting.

"Can I introduce my fiancé, Jack Cooper?" she said to Robert. Her mother came into the room at that instant holding a dish of peanuts. "Oh, I've already introduced them," she said cheerfully. "They've been having a great argument."

"About what?"

"Commerce."

"The role of the big internationals in the economy," said Robert smoothly. "I think we agreed to differ."

"It sounds very important."

"Oh, it was," said Jack. "Very important, world shattering."

Anne excused herself and went into the kitchen to attend to the roast. Jack followed her out of the room.

"You weren't really arguing?" she asked.

"Of course not. He was being a bit

pompous so I couldn't resist taking him down a peg or two. These big business men always annoy me, think they know it all just because they've made a bit of bread."

"I don't think Robert Fordham's pompous," Anne said. She would have described him as anything but pompous. "Be nice to him," she said. "I don't want to upset Mother."

"I am being nice to him," Jack said, "tell *him* to be nice to *me*. He isn't the King of Siam, after all, even though your mother thinks he is."

However, there were no more arguments, barbed or otherwise, but gentle discussions on safe subjects, and the meal progressed satisfactorily.

"When are you two getting married?" Robert asked at one point.

"They haven't set the date," said Barbara Tyson quickly, "I want to get all my business affairs settled before I can deal with a wedding."

"But you're not getting married, Mrs. Tyson dear," said Jack. Barbara flashed an enigmatic look at him. "Weddings take a lot of preparation," she said.

"What about sometime in June, Anne darling?" Jack suggested.

"Very traditional," Barbara said, "but it's too near, won't give me time to get organised. Sarah was married in June, of course, and we had a big marquee on the lawn."

"Oh, I don't want a big wedding like Sarah's," said Anne quickly. "Just a few friends."

"I'm afraid we can't have just a few friends," said her mother. "We know too many people and too many people would be offended if they weren't asked. We asked everyone to Sarah's—friends, relatives, all the work people at the factory . . ."

"I feel like rushing off to a registry office at the thought of it," Anne shuddered.

"No, no," Barbara said quickly. "We'll compromise somehow, won't we, Jack? What do you want to do?"

"I'm easy," Jack said. "I have a lot of friends in London who'll probably want to come—but I have no family except some remote cousins whom I never see."

"And your daughter Karen," Anne thought to herself, but did not say aloud. She had not yet told her mother that Jack had been married before. Somehow she would face that hurdle later. Her mother was being so agreeable to him that she did not want to spoil things.

"Well, you must talk it over together," Barbara Tyson said, "and let me know what you want to do in plenty of time. But quite honestly, I think you should resign yourselves to a big do and have a decent send-off."

After dinner, while they were drinking their coffee, Barbara turned to Robert and said, "I've had some plans made about a possible extension of the bakehouse. Would you like to see them?" and when he agreed, she got up and said, "Come into my study. I've got a big desk and we can spread them out."

Anne and Jack were left alone. They were sitting companionably on the sofa and Jack put his arms around her and began kissing her.

"Please," she said, "Please, they'll be coming back in a moment. Please let me go."

"Why?" he asked roughly. "We're going to get married, aren't we? Why do you fight me off all the time?"

"I don't know. Please be patient, Jack. I feel in such a muddle."

He began kissing her again more roughly than before, taking no notice of her protests but at last, aware of her distress, he let her go reluctantly. She smoothed down her hair. "It's not the time or place," she said breathlessly.

"It never is the time or place."

"I'm sorry." She put out her hands to make amends but he pushed her away impatiently.

"I do love you, you know," she said.

"Yes, yes, and I love you too."

They heard the voices of her mother and Robert. They were coming back. When they came into the room, Anne was pouring herself some more coffee and Jack was looking at a magazine. He threw it aside. "It's time I went," he said. "Thank you for a lovely evening." He bowed formally to Barbara and nodded at Robert. Anne followed him into the hall. He bent down and kissed her perfunctorily.

"I'll see you tomorrow?" she asked tentatively.

"Probably. I'll phone you." He put his

face to hers, "Don't worry so, Anne. Everything will be all right."

When she rejoined her mother and Robert, they were talking about the coming weekend, the weekend Barbara and Anne were going to stay with James Millard at Sorrel Place.

"You're going to be there?" Barbara asked Robert.

"Oh, yes." He turned to Anne. "Would you like me to get James to include your fiancé in the invitation? I'm sure he would be very happy to."

Before she could speak, Barbara broke in, "I think we had better leave it as it is. After all, James asked us some time ago and he's probably made all his arrangements, and I'm sure Jack will understand, won't he, Anne?"

"Of course."

"It is, after all, a kind of working weekend," Barbara went on. "We are going to talk a lot of shop and Jack would be terribly bored."

Robert laughed. "I don't think James is thinking of it as a working weekend but one devoted to pleasure and in showing off his beautiful house."

6

JACK was not pleased to hear she was going away for the weekend.

"I'm sorry, darling," Anne said, "I don't want to go either but we're staying with the man who is buying us out."

"I should have thought I could be invited along too," Jack said. Anne was silent. She did not say Robert Fordham had offered to suggest just such a thing and that her mother had vetoed it.

"You'd only be bored if we talk *Grandma Tyson* all the time," Anne said more cheerfully than she felt.

Jack's mood changed suddenly. He laughed "I guess so, but aren't you thrilled that *Grandma Tyson* will soon be behind you and that you won't have to worry about those footling biscuits any more?"

"I haven't made my mind up yet," Anne said carefully.

"Then I shall make it up for you," said Jack gaily, "and plan our trip round the world to all those faraway romantic places.

Our honeymoon trip. Which is it to be first? India or China? Or should we just settle for the South of France?"

Anne's mood lightened to match his. Of course, he was not serious. He knew how much her job had meant to her.

"Well, I can't leave straight away," she said. "There'll have to be a replacement for me."

"And that'll be hard to find, my darling," said Jack "I should think you're just about irreplaceable."

"No one's that," said Anne.

"Well, you are, to me." He drew her into his arms and began kissing her, methodically and expertly, taking her breath away. She pulled away first, as always, trying to keep her self-control. He watched her push her hair back from her brow, a curious light in his eyes. She would almost have said it was calculating except that was not a word to apply to Jack. He was the least calculating of men.

"You're an old-fashioned girl, aren't you?" he said. "Would you like a nightcap?"

Disappointed that he had stopped kissing her, not liking being called old-fashioned,

Anne sighed. "I must go home," she said. "It's late and we're making an early start in the morning. Mother wants us to get there for lunch."

"Run away if you must," Jack said. "I'll be patient."

Anne cupped his face in her hands. "You're very sweet to me," she said, "to bear with my silliness. You know I love you. Sometimes I feel I'm on the bank of a deep river, and if I jump in I'll drown."

"You should come on in, the water's fine," he said and dropped a kiss on the end of her nose. "Now run off home before I lose my patience and ravish you."

Both Anne and her mother overslept the next day and did not set out for the south as early as they had intended. Barbara made a telephone call to tell their host they would be with him for tea not lunch. The day was fine, the sun was shining and, this done, they set off down the motorway in good heart.

James Millard's directions had been detailed and explicit. He had sent them a carefully drawn map. They left the motorway as he directed and cut across country and some four-and-a-half hours after leaving home, they found themselves in the little village of Grayham.

"*Through the village and turn up the lane by the church,*" read out Anne from the instructions. "*Half a mile up the lane you will see the gates of Grayham.*"

The iron gates came into view. Large, imposing, black-and-gilded, the stone posts which supported them topped with heraldic beasts, they were open. They rattled across a cattle grid, up a winding drive bordered with shrubs, then they came out into open parkland, dotted with mature trees under which deer grazed, and far away in the distance, against a background of dark woods, a grey, many-windowed, square house came into view.

"My, my," Anne said.

Barbara stopped the car and they both stared, surprise making them silent.

"It's huge," Barbara said at last. "James said it was a small manor house. I didn't realise it would be quite so imposing."

"Well, I suppose it *could* be described as a manor house," said Anne doubtfully. "It's not *quite* as big as Chatsworth or Blenheim," she added and laughed. "Has

110

he lived here always? I mean is it a family home?"

"No, no," said her mother. "He's a self-made man. He bought it about twenty years ago. It was derelict, he told me, and he's been restoring it ever since. A family called Grayham lived in it for centuries until the last one, an old maid, died about 1958; it was empty for a long time and then he bought it together with the estate. It's his hobby, he told me, instead of golf." She laughed a little excitedly. "Oh, I do hope we're going to enjoy this weekend."

She started up the car again and they moved slowly on up the drive into the gravelled, weed-free sweep in front of the house. There were stone urns full of daffodils standing sentinel along the terrace and great sweeps of daffodils bloomed under the trees at the side of the house.

Barbara Tyson stopped the car and took a deep breath. Anne glanced curiously at her mother. That was almost a sigh. What exactly did this weekend mean to her mother? And the sale of *Grandma Tyson*? And James Millard?

Their host was standing waiting for them in the pillared portico of his mansion, a trim, fit-looking man in his fifties, with silvered hair and a fresh complexion. Anne guessed his hair had been red in his youth. He was still good-looking.

He came down the steps to meet them, arms held out in welcome, and an enormous smile on his face.

"Hello, hello," he cried. "How lovely to see you. And this must be Anne—how d'ye do, Anne—come along in! Aren't we lucky to have such splendid weather! I was hoping you would see Grayham looking its best."

They followed him into the house. "Don't worry about your bags," he said. "Someone will see to them."

They came into a big square hall of breathtaking beauty. Stone-floored, its walls and sweeping curved ceiling were decorated in pale blue and white with painted arabesques and garlands and medallions.

"James Wyatt," James Millard said briefly, noticing Anne staring around her.

From arched doorways two other people appeared, Robert Fordham and a girl, dark-haired and beautiful.

"This is Natalie, my daughter, who

keeps house for me," James Millard said, "and, of course, you know Robert."

Natalie held out a languid hand. "How do you do?" she said, showing her small white teeth in a polite smile. Her hand was very cold and smooth. Her nails were beautiful, long and red-enamelled, Anne noticed in that brief moment.

Robert Fordham was more warm and welcoming. He asked them all the usual questions about their journey, smiled and seemed generally pleased to see them.

Anne surprisingly found herself pleased to see him. He seemed cosy and familiar somehow in these far from cosy and familiar surroundings.

"Now how about some tea?" James asked.

"It's all ready in the drawing-room," his daughter said, "but wouldn't Mrs. Tyson prefer to see her room first?"

The bags were being brought in by a man and a woman, obviously servants and obviously foreign.

"Yes, yes, of course." James turned to the woman. "Maria, show my guests their rooms, and perhaps Arlindo will take the car round to the garage." He looked enquiringly at Natalie.

"Mrs. Tyson is in the Rose Room, Miss Tyson next door," she said.

Looking down at her suitcase which seemed to have become smaller and shabbier on the journey, Anne had a momentary feeling of panic. Had she brought the right clothes? And enough of them?

Barbara gave the car keys to the smiling Arlindo and then they followed Maria, the maid, up the wide curving staircase into a long gallery. Huge windows lined one wall and a row of beautiful mahogany doors the other. In between the doors were oil-paintings depicting the seasons as four beautiful women attended by cherubs.

Their bedrooms were adjoining, with a bathroom in-between which they were evidently to share.

"I would have thought to have my own bathroom at least," said Anne to her mother.

"Oh Anne dear, you know how very quick I always am in the bathroom, it's no hardship to share."

"Oh, Mother!" Anne said "I was making

a joke. Next time I shall run up a little flag and say 'Joke coming!'"

Barbara gave a little forced laugh. "Silly of me," she said.

Anne plopped a kiss on the top of her head. Her mother, she guessed, had been as surprised and overwhelmed as she was by the opulence of their surroundings.

She washed her hands and face, combed her hair, renewed her make-up and, metaphorically squaring her shoulders, went downstairs again with her mother.

Maria was waiting at the foot of the stairs to show them the drawing-room.

The drawing-room was forty feet long and about twenty feet wide. Yellow silk hung in festoons at the long windows over-looking the park and terrace. Anne was aware of a multitude of pictures on the panelled walls, a beautiful Aubusson on the polished floor, exquisite furniture ranged about. At the far end was a tea-trolley, covered with a white lace cloth, and presiding over the tea-cups and pouring out of the silver tea-pot was Natalie. Sitting around her were her father and Robert and another man whom James introduced to them as Nick Hillman, "Natalie's friend".

Nick was fair and pleasant-faced and friendly, handed them their tea-cups and passed the cucumber sandwiches and the iced cakes with alacrity.

Anne found herself on a sofa sitting beside Robert Fordham. "You should have warned me," she said, "I didn't know we were coming to a palace."

Robert looked at her quizzically. "James loves his surprises," he said. "I wouldn't have spoilt it for him for the world. This house is his pride and joy. I believe it was practically falling down when he bought it, full of wet rot and dry rot and woodworm and with no roof in places."

"Oh, Robert," Natalie interrupted, "that was years ago. It's been like this ever since I can remember." She turned to Anne and said kindly, "Of course, if you're used to a much smaller house, it does seem large, but it is not all that big, you know. The rooms are large but there are not many of them. There was a great big Victorian addition which my father pulled down to make the house more manageable. Robert tells me you live on a little farm near your mother's factory?"

"Yes," said Anne.

"A very beautiful place," Robert said quickly, "As beautiful as this in its own way."

Anne smiled at him, maliciously pleased at his apparent discomfiture. "It *is* small and it is near my mother's factory," she said. "Your description is perfect."

Robert looked at her, his eyes alight with amusement. "You're deliberately misunderstanding," he said.

"Do you walk to work?" Natalie asked in the same kind tone. "Isn't it a bit of a bore being so near the factory?"

Anne turned her attention to her. "It is not as near as all that, and no, the factory is never a bore."

"Have you decided you're going to work for me?" Robert asked.

"*For* you?" Anne stressed the word. "I thought I was going to work *with* you."

"With or for, it's the same thing."

"Not quite." They stared at each other.

"I want you to work *with* me," Robert said softly. "I want you on my side, and I don't think you are—yet. I think you regard me as the enemy."

Anne laughed. "You flatter yourself. I haven't thought about you in any way at all," she lied. "But I need time to get used to the sale of *Grandma Tyson*."

"*Grandma Tyson* still needs you," Robert said. "We—I—want you very much to carry on—at least for the first few months till we get into our stride. The other evening when we were talking, I felt you weren't aware of how much you were needed."

"Because you're going to be very much tied up with your project at Hunthorpe?" Anne asked. "You won't have much time to spare for *Grandma Tyson?*"

"Now I think your claws are showing," Robert said. "You *do* think of me as the enemy. Obviously, Hunthorpe comes into it. I am going to have to work hard there but I have a broad back. I won't be overwhelmed if I have to take on *Grandma Tyson* too, but I don't want there to be even a hiccough when she comes under the wing of Warings. You can help." He put out his hand and patted hers. "Please. There, isn't that asking nicely?"

Anne laughed. "Too nicely. I'm very suspicious."

Natalie, noticing Robert's gesture,

interrupted again. "Robert, would you like some more cake?"

"No, thank you, but perhaps Anne would?"

James Millard and her mother had walked over to one of the windows and were looking out. James was waving his arms about, obviously pointing out various details on the view in front of them. They turned away from the window and James said they were going on a tour of the house. Would anyone else like to come? What about Anne?

Anne agreed politely that she would love to look over the house. Robert got up from the sofa and said he would come too.

"Oh Robert," Natalie exclaimed. "You said you would play tennis after tea."

"Play with Nick," Robert suggested. "I'll join you later. Maybe Anne would make a four?"

Anne declined. "I haven't played tennis for years," she said "I'll be a ball-boy."

They followed James and her mother out of the room. James Millard was a good guide. He loved his subject and he had spent hours researching the history of the house, its succession of owners, the artists and craftsmen who had worked on it. Barbara Tyson listened, absorbed.

Anne, less interested, found her attention wandering. Instead, she thought about the man at her side, Robert Fordham. The enemy indeed. He was too quick and perceptive. Did she want to go on working—with him, for him? He was charming and agreeable now, but somehow she felt that was only a façade. There was a steel core. It was conceivable they would not get on.

The object of her thoughts broke into her reverie. "Some time during this weekend, I want to talk to your mother about an office," he said.

Barbara overheard him. She turned away from the oil-painting she had been admiring. "Anything to do with the office is Anne's pigeon from now on," she said. "I am retiring gracefully. Anne is taking over—she might as well start now."

Robert looked down at Anne. "How about it?" he asked "Could you spare a small space for a desk for me? I shall be spending a lot of time in Hunthorpe in the near future."

"Won't you have something on the site?"

"Yes, but I would also like something at *Grandma Tyson's*. It would be more convenient to have the amenities of your office. A desk, a telephone maybe."

"Two telephones surely? And a secretary? Or perhaps a personal assistant and a secretary?"

"How very accommodating you are," Robert said smoothly, ignoring her half-joking sarcasm. "No, only a desk and a telephone, and of course you will be there to give me your very valuable advice."

Barbara, half-listening to James, half to their conversation, came in at the tail end: "Oh Robert, you will find Anne is absolutely invaluable. She knows more than I do about *Grandma Tyson*. She has brilliant ideas, she works fantastically hard . . ."

"Please, Mother!" Anne protested. "Are you giving me a reference?" She turned to Robert, ready to say anything to shut her mother up. "Of course you can have a desk in our office. I'll get Beryl to find you a corner somewhere."

James and Barbara had moved across the picture gallery into another room and were out of sight.

"Mother and your boss seem very friendly—I mean, more than this business of *Grandma Tyson* seems to warrant," Anne said.

Robert was a little slow in answering and then he said, "The business brought them together but James is certainly very taken with your mother. I have never seen him go overboard before. In fact, I have never seen him overboard. It took him a long time to get over the death of his wife. She died when Natalie was about three and he has wrapped himself up in his daughter, his work and this house, in that order, with no room for anyone or anything else. He is a very warm, loving man, Anne. Your mother could do a lot worse."

"Do you suppose they are going to get married?" Anne asked.

Robert seemed surprised at her question. "Hadn't you better ask your mother?" They were standing by one of the long windows in the gallery and Robert looked out across the park. "Anyway, why should you mind if your mother gets married? Aren't you getting married yourself to that lucky man, Jack?"

"I don't mind," Anne said defensively.

"It just explains things a little better to me."

"And you? You are getting married how soon, Anne? I don't want to start depending on you and then have you whisked away."

"*If* I go on working for *Grandma Tyson,*" Anne said slowly and carefully, "I won't get whisked away. I am pretty conscientious." She did not look at him but out at the burgeoning countryside, thinking with one part of her how lush and rich it all looked. Would all this magnificence seduce her mother?

"'Pretty' being the operative word," said Robert.

"I think 'conscientious' is the operative word," said Anne primly.

He laughed and she met his glance then, and they looked at each other for a long time without speaking as though searching for truth in each other's eyes.

Anne turned away first. "I feel so muddled," she said. "Everything is in such a state of flux and now this—Mother and James . . ."

"You have a choice," Robert said, "but it shouldn't be too difficult . . ."

Before he could finish his sentence he was interrupted. "Ah, there you are!" They turned to see Natalie. She was breathless as though she had been running. "Pa and Mrs. Tyson are downstairs. I thought you must be lost." She looked from one to the other with bright inquisitive eyes.

"How could I get lost?" Robert asked easily "I know my way around."

"Well, are you coming to play tennis?" Natalie caught hold of his hand. "Come on!"

Robert allowed himself to be led away and Anne followed more slowly. She wasn't absolutely sure what Robert felt about Natalie but it was pretty obvious what Natalie felt about Robert. He was her property and if she had held up a little placard with *Hands off!* printed on it, she could not have made herself clearer. She must wave her engagement ring in front of Natalie sometime to assure her that she wasn't in the least bit interested in Robert Fordham other than as a business partner, and that her heart lay elsewhere.

When Anne got downstairs, it was to find Nick Hillman waiting for her.

"Would you like a swim?" he suggested.

"But don't you want to play tennis?"

He shrugged. "Not specially. A threesome's rather boring and I'm not going to be used as a stalking horse by Natalie. I don't know why she asked me this weekend if she's going to fawn all over Robert Fordham all the time. I'd rather keep you company."

"I didn't bring a swimsuit."

"Not to worry. I'm sure our hostess can fit you up with something."

He took her out of the house through the gardens to a large, beautiful pool which had been made in what had obviously been an old sunken garden. It was surrounded by a well-trimmed box hedge, six feet high, thick, protective, and impenetrable. Mossy stone statues of various goddesses were spaced at intervals in niches cut into the box.

The pool, lined with deep blue tiles, was a beautiful curved shape with a marble surround. At one end there was a wider paved area with a little Greek pavilion with cane chairs and cushions.

On the surface of the water a small pancake-shaped object was scurrying about, keeping the water clean. As it moved from side to side, in its animated fashion, it was like some small, industrious, mysteriously-shaped animal. By the side of the pool there were various longhandled rakes and perforated spoon-shaped objects to collect leaves which might dare to fall in and sully the pristine crystal of the water.

"And frogs," said Nick. "The silly things dive in and drown. It's too deep for them. They get to the bottom and can't get up again. We have all mod cons. There's a jacuzzi at that end which will give you an underwater massage, but best of all, the water's heated! Let's find you something to wear, unless you wish to swim *au naturel*? I will if you will." He looked at her enquiringly.

"Not today."

He led her to the pavilion and in a cupboard they found a selection of swimsuits and bikinis to fit variously shaped figures. Anne was tempted by a pretty gold lamé bikini but in the end settled for a splashy orange-and-pink printed cotton one. In the pavilion there was a stereo, and Nick put on a cassette of Strauss waltzes before he dived into the water.

The sun was shining from a clear blue sky, the water was pleasantly warm, the music floated out in beautiful cadences. Anne suddenly felt exceptionally light-hearted, as though she hadn't a care in the world. She dived and floated, swam and splashed like a dolphin.

They were still in the water when Robert and Natalie appeared. The day seemed even brighter. "Why," thought Anne with surprise, "I must really like him," realising it was Robert who had this effect on the atmosphere.

"Come on in," she said. "The water's lovely and warm."

"Of course it is," Natalie said. "My father keeps it heated so that he can swim all the year round."

She and Robert joined them in the water. Natalie was slender and slim as a little elf. (She was wearing the gold lamé bikini, Anne noticed, glad she had left it.) Robert, strongly-built, with a well-muscled torso, looked a giant beside her. He dived in, a graceful racing dive which brought him within a few yards of Anne. He splashed her playfully and she splashed him back more relaxed than she had ever been with him.

She and Nick got out of the water before the other two. Anne stood for a moment on the side of the pool, wringing out her hair. She had not worn a cap or tied it up in a scarf and it was hanging in wet tails round her face. It must look terrible but she hated wearing a cap. Thank heaven she had brought some heated rollers with her which would help to make it look more presentable for this evening.

She was suddenly aware she was under observation and turned to see Robert and Natalie were staring at her. Robert's eyes quite deliberately raked her body from her head to her toes, as though examining her for some flaw. She could not fathom or understand the expression in them except it both disconcerted and irritated her.

Natalie's expression was easier to understand. It was not admiring but a sour mixture of envy and dislike. Anne was equally disconcerted by it and felt like telling her she was a stupid little girl. With all she had, and her undoubted beauty, there was no need for her to be envious of anyone.

Anne knew her figure was good but it was not something she was vain about. She had been lucky enough to be born with it. She wasn't particularly athletic; she didn't have to diet; she ate what she liked and her waist and hips stayed trim.

She shook more water out of her hair, turned her back on them both and walked proudly back to the pavilion where she found Nick waiting for her with towels and a towelling robe to wrap herself in, which she did very quickly. The pool was protected from any breeze but the air seemed to be getting a little chillier as the sun was setting.

Robert and Natalie came out of the water almost at once. Natalie was panic-stricken. "I've just remembered. There are people coming for drinks," she said. "They will be here in less than an hour."

"My hair!" thought Anne and then relaxed. What did it matter if her hair was wet? It was not the end of the world.

"I've got a hair-dryer," Natalie said to Anne as though she had read her mind.

"Thank you," Anne shrugged. "I shall just have to have wet hair."

7

ANNE met her mother coming out of her bedroom as she rushed into her own to change her clothes and do something about her wet hair.

"Wherever did you get to?" her mother asked, turning back. She sat on the bed while Anne vigorously towelled her hair. There was a knock on the door and Maria appeared with the hair-dryer from Natalie.

"Oh, how marvellous," Anne cried, taking it from her. "Please thank Miss Natalie for me." She found a convenient plug near the dressing-table and began to blow dry her long, wet locks.

"We went swimming," she said, "a simply gorgeous pool. Natalie forgot there were people coming."

"She's a beautiful girl," her mother said inconsequentially.

"Does she live with her father in London?" Anne asked.

"She does, but she's been in America these past few months so I haven't met her before. What about this house, Anne? Isn't it fabulous? What do you think of James?"

"Very charming," Anne said, "and his house is magnificent."

She waited for her mother to confide in her but the older woman was silent. She got up from the bed and walked over to the window and looked out. "I had better go down," she said after a moment. "These people are arriving any minute. See you downstairs, darling."

Anne slipped out of her slacks and shirt and zipped herself into a dress of finely-pleated silk in a dark Paisley design, more suitable for drinks and dinner. She clipped gold earrings in her ears, and fastened a thick gold chain round her neck. She looked at herself in the mirror. Her hair was still damp but it had regained some shape. She looked well enough, she supposed, not noticing the brightness of her eyes, the bloom of her skin.

When she got downstairs, it was to find a dozen or so people in the drawing-room. Robert detached himself from the couple he was talking to and came forward and introduced her to Colonel and Mrs. Sparling, some of James's neighbours. He took her round the room, introducing her to everyone.

"And now," he said, the introductions over "what will you have to drink?" Arlindo appeared magically at his elbow with a tray of assorted glasses, full of glittering liquids, varying from colourless to pale gold and amber—gin, wine, sherry, whisky. Anne took a glass of wine.

"Ah," said James, "you're doing my job, thank you, Robert."

Her mother was standing with a little group of people and James rejoined them. More people arrived and James went forward this time and brought them into the room and introduced them to Barbara. She was the honoured guest, Anne noticed. This little party seemed designed around her. Her mother, flattered by all the attention, looked her prettiest.

Eventually, there were about thirty people in the room. Anne met them all and they were friendly and polite, asking the usual questions that people ask at cocktail parties—where she lived—what she did—how long she was staying—but they all knew each other and so sometimes their attention was distracted from her while they greeted old friends. She was detached, a little apart, watching, as only an outsider can. She noticed how helpful Robert was, acting almost as a son of the house, although Nick, her fellow guest, also did his bit in getting people drinks and passing round the canapés. He also hovered comfortingly round her, giving her potted biographies of the people present under his breath. He apparently had been brought up about twenty miles away, where his parents still lived, although he lived and worked in London.

"A pillar of the church and the WI," he muttered as a large lady in a purple dress bore down on him with an empty glass. "Keep a riding stable," he said as a dapper young couple helped themselves to sausages.

Robert too saw that she was not neglected." Your hair looks beautiful," he said. "I don't know how you girls do it. No one would think Natalie has been swimming either."

"But her hair is short," said Nick, "not like the mermaid's here." Both men stared at her and Anne shook her head, smiling at their compliments.

"You're too kind," she said, not believing a word they said, just thinking they wanted to please.

Natalie came up at that moment. She linked her arms into the arms of both men. "Sorry, Anne, I must take them away. There's someone over there who wants to talk to Robert and Mrs. Franks hasn't got a drink." Robert cast a rueful look in her direction as he was borne away. Anne was left alone again. Yes, Natalie was very much the hostess, but her mother was the star guest. James presented people to her as if she were the Queen.

The party broke up promptly around eight-thirty and everybody left. "There must be something on the telly they want to watch," said James as they went into the dining-room to eat.

This room was slightly smaller than the drawing-room, papered in a rich, ruby-red flock paper, hung with portraits, a beautiful landscape over the chimneypiece and pier glasses between the long windows.

The glossy mahogany table was set with silver candelabra and a beautiful arrangement of spring flowers—freesia mixed with narcissi—and their sweet scent hung on the air.

Natalie sat at one end of the table, her father at the other with Barbara on his right and Anne on the other side. For a few minutes, the talk was general while James explained who all his guests had been. He turned to Barbara. "We have a very pleasant community here," he said, "I think you would like it. I have very many congenial friends."

"They all seemed charming," Barbara agreed.

"Of course, I imagine this part of the world is not as rural as yours," James went on, "We are too near London and perhaps a little bit urban for your taste?"

Barbara laughed. "There is nothing urban about Grayham," she said. "It is like I have always imagined a true, old-fashioned English country house should be—beautiful gardens, conservatories, objects, paintings—" she paused.

Robert continued for her "But much more comfortable than most old-fashioned country houses," he said "Warmer—and with no inconvenient draughty bath-rooms—"

"I have never been north," interrupted Natalie. "I always imagine it dark
and black and cold and wet."

"You are very ignorant, my dear," her
father said pleasantly. "I am afraid like
most of the young these days you know
other parts of the world better than your
own country. You spend holidays in
France, Italy, America, winter in
Switzerland—it's time you travelled
around England."

Natalie pulled a little face. "I like the
sun," she said.

"Well, the sun does shine in our part of
the world too," Anne said.

"When are you coming north?" Barbara
asked James quietly. "When are you
coming to look at your new acquisition?"

"I'm coming next week sometime."

"I hope you will stay with us," Barbara
said.

"Robert will be with me."

"Robert too. We will be delighted to
have him again."

"I can't impose on you," Robert said. "I
want to have quite a long visit this time. I
thought perhaps I could stay in a pub close
by."

"I shall be mortally offended if you don't stay with us," said Barbara smiling, "And you must stay as long as you want to."

"Can I come too?" asked Natalie.

"Why not? We have plenty of room," said Barbara equably. "Make your first visit north, and find out, it's not grizzly bear country. We'd love to have you all."

"Robert can drive me up," Natalie said, and when Robert was silent, she added, "You don't mind, do you?"

"Of course not."

"That's settled then."

Robert turned to Anne. "You sure it's not going to be too much for you and your mother?"

"No, no, we'd love to have you all."

After dinner, they took their coffee in the library, a big square room, its books arranged on old mahogany shelves. The furniture consisted of comfortable old leather chairs and sofas, a beautiful round leather-topped table, set with a collection of magazines and a large white cyclamen in a Crown derby *cache-pot*.

Natalie busied herself with the coffee-cups at one end of the room. Robert stood by her ready to hand them round.

James and Anne's mother were standing near the fireplace where a log fire burned. "They make a handsome couple, don't they?" James said fondly to Barbara, looking at his daughter and Robert. He spoke quietly but Anne, sitting on the sofa in front of the fire, heard him. "It is my dearest wish that they will get married soon," James went on. "Natalie hasn't been too careful in her choice of boyfriends in the past—but this time I think it will be different. Robert is a very fine man and very clever. I couldn't wish for a better son-in-law. He will keep Natalie in order. She can be very headstrong at times."

"I expect you have spoiled her," Barbara said lightly, "And why not? She is a very lovely girl. I didn't know that she and Robert . . ."

"Here's your coffee." Robert was in front of her, holding out a small gold cup. "Cream or sugar?"

Barbara shook her head. "Neither."

"So," thought Anne, "that is the way the land lies." Well, they did make a handsome pair, but she could wish for someone nicer for Robert. She must admit she didn't like Natalie very much. But perhaps it was rather unfair to make such a judgment on a day's acquaintance. She gave a small sigh. She did not suppose there would be any obstacles put in the way of their marriage. She looked up at her mother. "Why don't you sit down, Mother? You look a little tired." Her mother had gone rather pale, she noticed. She was possibly exhausted after all the excitement of the day.

The weekend continued to be both exciting and exhausting. James seemed determined that every minute of their time should be occupied.

Saturday they were taken shopping in the very pretty market town nearby, then to see the Castle, a local beauty spot and museum. At lunch, Natalie and Robert and Nick, who had forsworn the sightseeing, joined them at a pub in the town.

"Poor you!" said Natalie, plonking herself down between Robert and Nick. "Having to go round that dreary old museum. Daddy's quite gaga about it— probably likes to go and look at all the paintings and whatnots he's given it."

"It was very interesting," said Anne politely. She had enjoyed her morning. She had begun to see why her mother had been so charmed by James. He *was* charming and his enthusiasm about everything was very endearing. Nothing seemed too small to catch his attention; or too large either for that matter.

There had been no "shop" talk. As Robert had foretold, this visit was strictly for pleasure. In the evening, there was to be a dinner party—and on Sunday a lunch party before they drove home.

"I think I'm going to need another weekend to recover from the weekend," said her mother cheerfully.

"I am afraid my father *is* rather tiring," said Natalie, "if you're not used to a busy social life."

"I expect I'll survive," Barbara Tyson said a little drily.

Anne looked up from the menu she was studying to meet Robert's eyes. She could not read the expression in them—it was kind of considering and almost, you might say, wistful, as though he felt sorry for her.

"Are *you* going to survive?" he asked her. She felt the question had a deeper meaning than its surface one but she answered him lightly. Why should he feel sorry for her?

"Of course I am. I'm a survivor, didn't you guess?"

"I wouldn't dare to guess anything about you."

They were speaking quietly under the cover of the others' chatter about the dishes they were going to order. Anne had the strangest sensation that they were alone, in a foreign country, trying to communicate in a foreign tongue.

"I am very ordinary," Anne said. "All my reactions, my responses are run-of-the-mill . . ."

"You undersell yourself," he said.

"I shouldn't do that to you, I suppose," she said, "But there's no need to feel sorry for me."

"Who said anything about feeling sorry for you?" he asked in surprise.

Their attention was caught by James who wanted to know what they were going to eat, and there was no more talk between them. There was no more chance to talk as the weekend slipped away. Anne felt frustrated. She wanted to talk to Robert Fordham, naturally, to explain away the misconceptions he had about her. She wasn't a hysterical twit, or contrary, or temperamental as he seemed to infer. She tried to find an opportunity to talk to him, to be alone without an interruption, but it proved impossible. There were too many calls on his time from Natalie, and from James. And Nick Hillman danced too much attendance on herself. The fact that Nick ignored Natalie piqued the latter. Despite her preoccupation and open adoration of Robert, Natalie also wanted Nick's attention too. She was a very spoilt girl, Anne concluded, and had never been crossed in anything in her life.

Nick said as much to her when they were sitting together after dinner on a sofa in the drawing-room. The dinner party on Saturday night for twenty-four had been a mixture of Natalie's and her father's friends.

The "wrinklies", as Natalie insisted on calling the older guests, were now ensconced in the library at three bridge tables. Anne wondered how her mother was getting on. She didn't like bridge much and no one could class her as a "wrinkly".

The younger ones were in the drawing-room where one end had been cleared of furniture, and the floor of rugs, for dancing. Music was coming from an elaborate hi-fi hidden in an antique cabinet.

"She was always a horrid spoilt child," said Nick, "with too many Christmas presents and always the best and most expensive pony in the Pony Club—and then she grew up rather pretty."

"And you fell in love with her?" suggested Anne.

"Uh-huh!" Nick idly picked up her left hand.

"Why do you wear this ring?" he asked.

"For the obvious reason. I happen to be engaged to be married."

"You don't look engaged," said Nick.

"How should an engaged girl look then?"

"Oh, demure and dull. Not as kissable as you. Do you know I've been longing to kiss you all weekend—I've been seeking an opportunity—and I suppose I shouldn't and mustn't."

Before Anne could answer, he leaned forward and kissed her on the mouth, pressing her head back into the sofa cushions with his ardour.

He drew away from her after a few moments. Robert and Natalie were standing in front of them. Anne guessed he had seen them walk towards them and the kiss was for Natalie's benefit.

"Aren't you two going to dance?" asked Natalie, her eyes flashing.

"We're busy," said Nick.

"I can see you are, but come along, you've got to dance." She tried to pull Nick up from the sofa but he resisted and instead pulled her down on top of them. Natalie struggled to keep her balance but ended up in a heap between them, laughing.

Robert held out a hand to Anne. "Don't you want to dance?" They moved away but Natalie was up and after them in a second. It was Nick who put his hands on Anne's shoulders and staring intently into her face began swaying with her in time to the beat.

"Who's being used as a stalking horse now?" Anne asked. "Are you trying to make Natalie jealous?" She had been annoyed by Nick's kiss but what was the use of being irritated? She could wish that Robert Fordham had not been a witness. No doubt he would jump to all the wrong conclusions.

Driving away from Grayham after lunch on Sunday, Anne was certain of one thing.

James Millard was very much in love with her mother. Of her mother's feelings she was completely in the dark. Her mother was sweet, charming, admiring, agreeable to all suggestions but she gave no sign of any deeper emotion.

Several times during the weekend, Anne noticed Natalie glancing speculatively at her mother. She was glad, for pride's sake, that her mother was so calm, so self-possessed.

How was Natalie going to take this new interest in her father's life?

Had James declared himself in so many words? She was too shy to ask. It would be prying. On the journey home, they talked of James's house and his gardens and his beautiful possessions, but hardly at all about the man himself.

They talked a little of Natalie. Anne kept her reservations to herself. Her mother seemed to think Natalie was charming. "But making rather a fool of herself over Robert—but then she's very young. I'm quite sure there's no understanding there, whatever James thinks."

"But it would surely be very suitable? Robert is obviously the Crown Prince."

"Even James can't have everything his own way," her mother said cheerfully.

Of course, Anne thought to herself, she had been crazy to want to talk to Robert this weekend. There would be time enough in the coming weeks to get on terms with him, to explain herself, and disabuse him of all his preconceived ideas about her that had been the outcome of that unfortunate lunch and its humiliating sequel. She chided herself for thinking so much about him. He probably had not given her a second thought.

In the morning, going to work, Barbara said, "I really meant what I said about withdrawing, you know, Anne darling. I shall clear up my desk today. I thought Robert Fordham could possibly have my desk when he comes up tomorrow—"

"Tomorrow? But I thought they were all coming up later in the week."

"There was a change of plan. Didn't you hear them discussing it? Robert wants to get here as soon as possible so Natalie is coming up with her father—so I will have a lot to do in the house. I want to see that everything is perfect for them and Robert could use my office while he is working here."

In as much as she had thought about it at all, Anne had thought she herself would move into her mother's office. It was far more spacious and comfortable than her own small domain.

She took a deep breath. "Mother, I thought you told me that I was going to be in overall charge of *Grandma Tyson*."

Her mother looked at her in surprise. "But you are."

"Well, then, I think I should move into your office and Robert Fordham can use mine."

"We can't possibly put him in that little cubby-hole."

"I've been in it for some time past."

"But that's different," her mother protested.

"How so?"

"I'm not going to argue with you over such a trivial matter."

"Well then, if it's so trivial, it doesn't matter where Robert Fordham has his office."

"Oh, Anne darling, what's come over you? Don't be so exasperating," Barbara

Tyson cried. "We can't possibly put Robert in your office. It's too small. He will be offended. If you insist on having mine, we'll give him a desk in there."

"I am not sharing an office with Robert Fordham," Anne said. "Why should I? He already thinks of me as a nonentity—a mere cog in the machine. He knows I was not privy to the sale. He has to learn that I am not going to share the management of *Grandma Tyson* with him. Or I shan't stay."

"I didn't know Robert's opinion of you was so important to you."

"It's not his opinion I care about—it's my own position."

Barbara Tyson was silent, staring at her intransigent daughter in a kind of admiring dismay.

"You must do as you think best," she said at last. "But I really think your attitude is extremely petty."

"How long is he going to stay with us?" Anne asked.

"How should I know? I suppose until he finds somewhere to live."

Rumours had got around the factory of the proposed sale of *Grandma Tyson's* to Warings—or merger, as it was rather importantly called by the deputation of anxious men who called to see Barbara as soon as she arrived at the factory that morning.

"Your jobs will be perfectly safe," she assured them. "Safer, in fact, under the enormous umbrella of Warings. It is a huge, powerful combine and all its employees are treated handsomely. There's an excellent pension scheme . . ."

"We have an excellent pension scheme here, Mrs. Tyson," said the chief spokesman, a grizzled old man who had been in charge of the ovens since she first began production twenty years ago. He pushed his white cap further back on his head. "I understand you're leaving the firm."

Barbara laughed. "Well, the news certainly does get around fast. Wherever did you hear that? Yes, I am leaving in a way, I suppose, but I'm giving up my position to my daughter here. I shall still be taking an interest, all the same, but my daughter is going to take over my job. There's still going to be a Tyson looking after your interests in the factory itself. Everything will continue exactly the same as before—we are just going to have access to greater markets, greater means of distribution and supply—to become even more successful . . ."

They all went away quite happy in the end, relieved of the worry which was uppermost in their minds, losing their jobs.

"You see, Anne, you've *got* to stay when I leave," Barbara Tyson said, "at least for a year, until the take-over is going smoothly. I don't want to let anyone down."

"Neither do I," said Anne slowly, touched by the relief they had shown when they heard she was to remain as head of the business. She and Jack would work something out. He had said he could work anywhere. She rang him a couple of times during the day but there was no answer.

Her mother, after clearing out her desk, and taking a pile of papers home, had left early. She had plans for making herself a study-office at Lowater. "Beryl can work for us both," she said. "I can't part with her entirely. There's all my personal correspondence to see to . . ."

"I don't know why you have to be in such a rush," protested Anne. "There's time yet to sort your desk out."

"A clean break," her mother said hurriedly. "I want to make a clean break now. I want you to deal with all the formalities in connection with Warings. You are the boss here now." There was something a little frenzied about her actions and Anne guessed that in her heart of hearts, she was perturbed about the step she had taken. But now, having decided, she did not want to prolong the agony.

Anne called at Cragfall on her way home. The fine weather they had enjoyed over the weekend had vanished and in its place had come rain. As she drove into the yard of Cragfall, everything dripped. The house was silent and locked up, adding to the melancholy. Myra and George must have taken the children off somewhere, surely not walking in this weather, although the weather never interfered with their nature studies.

She parked the car and climbed up the steps of the barn leading to Jack's quarters. She could hear the sound of music so Jack must be there. As she walked into the room however, she could see no sign of Jack, although the music from the stereo was blasting forth loud and clear.

In one corner of the huge barn, a blanket had been laid on the floor, and lying on the blanket was a girl in a black leotard, waving long, black-clad legs in the air in time to the music. For a moment Anne stared at her, astonished, as the long, pretty legs bent and turned this way and that. The girl had her back to the door but she became aware that she had an audience and suddenly twisted her head round, and then sat up when she saw Anne.

"Hi," she said in a friendly tone. She rose up from the floor and moved over to the stereo. She hobbled a little, Anne noticed, and was extremely skinny. The girl switched the machine off and silenced descended suddenly.

"You looking for Jack?" the girl asked. "I'm afraid he's not here. He's gone fishing. In this rain, can you imagine? But he said it's the best time. The fish will be rising. He's promised me some for my supper."

"You're staying here?" asked Anne uncertainly.

"I came for the weekend," the girl said. "Jack was a dear when he heard of my predicament—I'm a dancer and I've hurt my ankle—and he asked me to come up and stay as long as I like. I'm Margot Fratelli," she added, holding out her hand.

"I'm Anne Tyson," Anne said, shaking the proffered hand.

"I'm Margot Fratelli," the girl said again as though Anne ought to know the name. "You know, one of the ten Gold Leopards. We're often on TV and we've been on tour lately—I was in Manchester when my ankle went. I danced on despite the pain. We dancers are accustomed to pain. It's a frightful blow and I don't know how long I'm going to be out of action. We dancers are different from anyone else, dedicated, you know."

"Yes," said Anne, "Oughtn't you to be resting it?"

"I suppose so, but it gets so boring." Margot hobbled round the house, picking up a bright orange skirt which she fastened over the leotard, tying a band over her black curly hair. "Isn't this a fabulous place? I've never known Jack not to fall on his feet and this is really a nice little pad. Have you known him long? Do you live around here? Fabulous place. Aren't the

Brackens a dream? Quite mad, of course, with all this back-to-nature bit!"

"Where are they?" Anne asked when Margot finally drew breath.

"I don't know. I fell asleep this afternoon and they were gone when I was woken up by the telephone."

"You didn't answer it."

"What would be the point? I knew it wouldn't be for me. Can I give you a drink? I'm sure Jack's got some liquor stashed away somewhere."

"No thank you," Anne said quickly. "I must go. Will you tell him I called when you see him?"

She drove back home, her heart and head a mixture of feelings . . . hurt, puzzlement and irritation. She mustn't be unreasonable. Why should she be irritated because Jack was hospitable to an old friend? Why did he have to inform her of everything?

She remembered her mother's words about Jack. "He comes from a different milieu. What do you know about him? All you know is what he has told you himself. But he knows everything about you."

Margot was part of Jack's unknown life. Like his daughter, Karen.

Jack was on the telephone as soon as she set foot inside the house. "Darling, I'm so sorry I missed you. You met Margot, I hear—"

"Yes."

"Are you all right? You sound funny somehow. You're not worried about Margot being here, are you? She's an old friend, having the most awful trouble with her boyfriend and now her ankle going wonky . . ."

"I was a bit surprised to see her, that's all."

"Yes, of course. But there's nothing to worry about. How did your weekend go?"

"Fine. We had a very nice time."

"Shall I drive out to see you this evening?"

"We've got a lot to do, Jack. Robert and the Warings, father and daughter, are coming to stay and I think my mother will need some help with the beds and things. Also we're both rather tired."

"See you tomorrow then?"

"I'll ring you."

But Jack came round to see her in the

office the next day and explained about Margot.

"She invited herself," he said. "I couldn't turn her down. She was rather depressed. What are friends for? You're not jealous, are you?"

Anne was silent for a few moments, considering. No, she thought, surprising herself, I'm not jealous. Was she that sure of Jack?

"I don't think so." she said. "Should I be?"

"There's no need to be jealous of Margot. You shouldn't have gone off on that jaunt to Grayham, leaving me all alone," Jack said. "Did you enjoy yourself?"

"It was very pleasant."

"And you didn't think of me, mooning about here on my own?"

"But you weren't on your own," Anne said, but of course she knew guiltily that she hadn't thought much about Jack during the weekend. There was too much else to claim her attention. The extraordinary surroundings. James, of course, and his daughter Natalie; not Eve, but a little serpent she feared in that Eden. And then there was the flirtatious Nick. And last, but not least, Robert Fordham. She did not know what adjectives to use for Robert— puzzling, elusive—no, aggravating—that was the best word.

8

ALTHOUGH Barbara Tyson could not hope to emulate the magnificence of James's hospitality, she was determined that hers would be no less generous or welcoming. So in the next day or so there was a polishing and refurbishment and arranging of flowers and food around Lowater which left Anne bemused and not a little impatient.

Robert Fordham arrived in the middle of it all, a day earlier than James and Natalie. It was left to Anne to settle him in his office, her former cubby-hole, and introduce him to Beryl.

Anne had cleared her desk, removed all her things to her mother's far roomier furniture, taken her files away from the bookshelves. The small office had been cleaned and dusted. Beryl had put a welcoming vase of narcissi on the desk. Robert seemed satisfied with all the arrangements made for him and Anne thought wryly of "the battle of the office"

159

as she termed it. So far, he had taken no offence.

"You seem a little harassed," Robert said when she and Beryl had finished showing him around. "I hope I'm not being a nuisance."

"Of course not," Anne said, not liking being called harassed. "I'm afraid my mother's making rather a production of this visit from James and we've all been a bit rushed. She wants everything to go smoothly."

"I'm sure it will," Robert said. "She tells me that you have decided to stay on after all. For at least a year."

"Yes."

"I'm very glad."

Anne busied herself with some papers on her desk. The glance from his grey eyes unnerved her. She did not know what was the matter with her. His presence in her mother's office—she must remember that it was now hers—also unnerved her as though he were an ogre or a monster to be placated. She felt that under his regard she was going to do everything wrong.

Robert drew out the chair at her mother's desk. "Now stop fiddling with those papers," he said, "and sit down." He caught hold of her by the elbow and steered her to the chair. "I want to talk."

Here was the opportunity she had wanted all weekend but somehow she could not take advantage of it. "What do you want to talk about?" she asked, still standing up.

"You," he said unexpectedly. "Please sit down, Anne. You unnerve me standing there looking so fierce, like a fire-eating dragon." Anne sat down and he sat himself opposite her across the littered expanse of the desk.

"We've never had a proper talk," Robert went on, "about you, I mean, unless you count that first lunch," he added softly "and that wasn't only about you but about me, too." He paused a moment. "I thought we had established some understanding then," he said. "Got to first base, as it were. Do you play baseball?"

Anne laughed involuntarily, "You know I don't."

"I mustn't use these Americanisms then. How nice to see you smile, Anne. Do you know you were glowering at me all weekend?"

"I was not!"

"That is, when you were not smiling sweetly at Nick Hillman," added Robert teasingly.

"I think Nick had his own reasons for being so gallant," said Anne "and they were nothing to do with me."

"You seem very certain."

"I think he is very interested in Natalie," said Anne boldly. If Robert could tease, so could she. "But he found he had too much competition from you."

"Ah, yes, dear little Natalie." His eyes glinted as he looked across the desk at her. "A mere child."

"I don't think Natalie thinks of herself as a child."

"It's how I think of her." His tone was dismissive. "I like a little more maturity in my women."

His women indeed. "You sound as if you have a harem."

"Oh, I do, I do."

"What do you want to know?" Anne asked ignoring this.

"About you?" Robert studied her gravely. "Lots of things, but for the

162

moment, I'd like you to describe your job here."

"I'm in charge of personnel," Anne said, "but that makes it sound more official than it actually is. I know it's corny but we *are* like a family. We're a very small firm and most of our people have been working for us for years, sometimes whole families, and we know all their histories and family events. So I look after all that side. Some of it, I suppose, can be classed as welfare work."

"And your mother has done the marketing?"

"I have helped her with that, too. In fact, I have helped her in various ways although she has always been in control of the everyday running of the factory. It's all been a very intimate business and I think a lot of our workers have felt a personal stake in things. I hope none of that is going to change."

"Why should it?"

Anne hesitated. "Warings is so huge and can't help but be impersonal."

"Not as impersonal as all that. It is run by people after all, not a computer. We look after our workforce, you know. What other of your worries can I demolish? I want to see you smile again, Anne."

Anne smiled despite herself. "You are ridiculous. Why should I glower at you?"

"Why indeed? I am the most amenable and gentle of men but you—you're as prickly as a hedgehog. Shall I tell you what I think? I think in your heart of hearts you're not reconciled to the sale of *Grandma Tyson* to Warings—that I—as the bearer of bad tidings, like the messengers of old, get most of the blame for it—"

"That's not so at all," cried Anne. "I am quite reconciled to it . . . I just don't want —I just don't want things to change too much," she added in a rush.

"Things will have to change," he said gently. "That is part of the price you have to pay for progress. I'll try and make it as painless for you as I can."

He looked away from her for a moment. "What else can I say to reassure you?"

"You could go away," Anne said to him silently, "and let us forget Warings and making our fortune—" and as these thoughts came into her head, they were succeeded by others. Truthfully, she would not like him now to go away. She was too

164

intrigued by him, too curious as to the changes he proposed for *Grandma Tyson*; in some contradictory way, too excited by all the recent events. She suddenly realised that her life would seem very tame if Robert Fordham walked out of it now. She was in some danger of becoming obsessed by him, she recognised with perception. She was too aware of him. She was irritated that he affected her so much. He, on the other hand, was so much in command of himself. Oh yes, he paid her pretty compliments and flattered her with his attention and his eyes, but she felt it was all an act, calculated to smooth his path in Warings' acquisition of *Grandma Tyson*.

She would like to make him angry, make him conscious of her as a person aside from *Grandma Tyson's* concerns, ruffle his smooth, suave exterior—bring him to heel, in other words. She smiled at this last thought. He was the last man in the world to be brought to heel and yet there would be a great deal of pleasure in his subjugation.

"What are you smiling at?" he asked.

"Am I smiling?"

"Like the Mona Lisa."

"At my thoughts."

"Secret ones?"

"I don't think you would like them anyway."

"Try me."

She shook her head.

He stared at her for a moment longer and then, understanding she was not going to tell him, he said, "Will you do something for me?"

"If I can."

"You *can* do an awful lot for me—if you *will*. I want you to make a list of all your employees and give me a run-down on every job. It'll take you quite a while so there's no need to rush at it. Let me have it early next week."

"It's a few hundred—" began Anne.

"So?"

Anne met his gaze across the desk. She wanted to ask him, if this was not rushing it, what was his idea of urgent, she wanted to say Warings have not taken over yet, but she did not want him to brand her as uncooperative right from the start.

"I'm jumping the gun a bit," Robert said, echoing her thoughts. "But we'll be having a time and motion study team here as soon as the formalities are completed and I want to be ready for them. I'm off to Hunthorpe now," he went on, "and I'll be there most of the day. Will Beryl take any messages for me?"

"Of course she will. Is there anything *more* I can do for you?" she asked sweetly, stressing the *more*.

He stared at her for a long time, silent, considering, and then he said, "Yes, there's quite a lot more, but I'll break you in lightly. I'm so relieved you're going to stay I don't want to spoil things. See you this evening." He patted her on the shoulder as he went out.

"He's rather nice, isn't he?" said Beryl, staring after him. "Very good-looking."

"Do you think so?"

"Smashing, and all the girls in the bakehouse think so too," she added. The office had a window which overlooked the bakehouse floor and several of the girls had left their tables and rushed to the windows to see Robert depart.

Anne gave a wry laugh. "We'll have to ask him to leave by another way if he's going to disrupt things like that."

Having Robert Fordham about the place

was going to be worse, much more agitating than she had feared. What was the matter with her? His presence seemed to take away her self-possession. There was a dynamism about him which she had never met in any man before. It was not his looks which impressed so much as his general presence. He would never be a man who was ignored or not remembered. But her mother had said that *she* was going to be in charge of *Grandma Tyson*, that they would be autonomous under the overall jurisdiction of Warings. She was not going to be bossed about like this by Robert Fordham. Somehow she would have to make her position clear. They had to work on equal terms.

9

"ISHALL just pray the weather's good," Barbara Tyson said, "and then we can have a nice tour round the Lakes and show him the countryside. The scenery can do my work for me. Everything's going to be very simple."

"Everything I am sure will be wonderful," Robert said easily, "James is a simple man at heart, you know. He will adore this place."

He and Barbara and Anne were sitting companionably after dinner in the small room which was known variously as the snug, the TV-room and the library according to whim. It fitted all these descriptions. The stove had been lit to take the chill out of the evening air and it was cosily warm. The next evening James and Natalie would be with them.

Barbara lay back in her chair, obviously well pleased with all her preparations. "I think I'm going to bed," she said.

"So early? It's only half-past nine," Anne

protested. As she was speaking, both dogs began to bark. With their keener hearing they had heard the sound of a car long before their owners.

Anne got up and switched on the outside and porch lights and opened the front door. It was a light, bright night and walking across the gravel drive, coming into the light, was Jack, followed by a well muffled hobbling figure she recognised as Margot Fratelli.

"Hello, hello," Jack gave her a boisterous hug. "It was such a lovely evening, we thought we'd come and take some coffee off you. Margot is dying to see Lowater Hall, I've talked so much about it."

Both of them followed Anne into the house, Margot squealing as she walked into the hall. "How gorgeous! What a darling place! How terribly old it must be! Oh, I do love all these beautiful colours, is your mother an artist?"

Bemused, Anne introduced her to Robert and her mother. Margot hobbled into the snug. "Oh, are we interrupting? Are you watching TV? Jack and I couldn't find anything we wanted to see . . . indescribably dreary . . ."

"Margot is staying with Jack," Anne explained to her mother. She had not thought it necessary to acquaint her mother with the news of Jack's strange guest before.

"I'm a dancer, you know," Margot said, "and I've had the most frightful accident —I've busted one of my ankles, or strained it or something—so what did I do, but call on dear Jack, as I have done a thousand times in my life, and he said life up here was a rest cure, and I can quite see it might be, especially in this wonderful dreamy place—" Without drawing breath, she turned to Robert, "And do you live here too? How simply marvellous!"

Like many people who talk a lot, she did not wait for answers to her questions, answering them herself as she went along.

"I'll get some more coffee," Anne said and fled to the kitchen. Jack followed her.

"I hope you didn't mind us barging in," he said, "but the Brackens are out and I thought Margot would burst if she didn't get out. She has a terrific amount of energy and this enforced idleness . . ."

"Yes, I know," Anne said, "she's a dancer."

Jack laughed. "Yes, she is, and rather a good one."

He helped her take the tray of coffee and cups back to the snug. Margot was sitting on the sofa next to Robert. He was staring at her in a mesmerised sort of way, as was Barbara in an easy-chair the other side of the stove.

Margot was not exactly pretty, Anne decided, looking at her. She had a long narrow face, topped with a shock of very black curls. She waved her long, thin hands about a lot as she talked. She was inclined to flop into a chair like a rag doll, an impression increased by her long attenuated legs. Tonight she was wearing a deep midnight blue full skirt topped with an enormous woollen sweater in pink, purple and brown and over that a huge Paisley shawl. It was warm in the snug and she gradually discarded shawl, then the sweater and finally appeared in a thin yellow shirt.

"Tell me what you do?" she said to Robert, fixing her bright black eyes on him.

"I work," he said. To Anne's eyes, he

appeared quite fascinated by this gypsy creature.

"Oh, so do we all. I'm a dancer," cried Margot "I'm with the Gold Leopards, you know, the TV dance troupe . . . ."

"I must go to bed," Barbara Tyson said. "Don't think me rude but I was going anyway before you came. I have had a hard day."

She made her good nights and left them.

The other three listened to Margot for the next half-hour and then Jack got up and said it was time they went.

"What a Christmas Tree!" said Robert when, finally, after a great many false starts, they had gone.

"Christmas Tree?"

"Yes, one of those women who wants everyone to dance around her." He yawned. "It's time we hit the hay too. The air gets me here, makes me sleep very well."

At the top of the stairs, he dropped a kiss on the top of her head as though she was a child. "Goodnight, Anne." He disappeared into his bedroom.

Despite the turmoil of her thoughts— Jack, Margot, Robert Fordham were all doing a dance in her head—or maybe because of them, Anne had no difficulty in falling asleep. She was off into the land of dreams as soon as her head hit the pillow.

She awoke with a sudden start. For a few seconds, she lay in her bed puzzled as to why she had awakened so suddenly. The old house creaked in the night, sometimes, and she listened but all was quiet. There was no wind and the silence was palpable. Then she heard a little tinkle as of a glass falling. There was another sound, a door shutting. She sat up. There was someone moving about downstairs. But why were the dogs so quiet? As usual they had been shut up to sleep in the kitchen. Had her mother been taken ill or something? She remembered Robert Fordham. Surely he wasn't wandering about in the middle of the night? She switched on her bedside light. It was one o'clock. She got out of bed and slipped on a dressing-gown and slippers and padded off down the stairs. She could see the kitchen light shining beneath the door, which was shut. She opened the door and peered fearfully round it.

Robert was kneeling by the sink brushing

a broken glass into a dustpan. His hair was ruffled and his bare legs and bare feet showed beneath a short, red check dressing-gown. He looked like a small boy caught in some shameful act.

"I'm terribly sorry," he said, "I've woken you up. I was looking for a glass. I wanted a drink of water."

"Oh, but there should be one and a carafe of water by your bed. How careless of us! Did you look in the bathroom?"

"No, I didn't," Robert said. "I came down here instead and practically got eaten by the dogs, and then I found a glass and dropped it on the flags."

"And that was the end of it!" said Anne. She opened a cupboard and found another glass. "Here's another one in case there isn't one in the bathroom. I can't understand why there wasn't one in your room after all the fuss Mother's been making. She even put a barrel of biscuits in James's room . . ." She chatted on nervously.

"Maybe James has got my glass too," said Robert. "I'm sorry to have disturbed you." There was a rueful expression in his grey eyes.

It was very quiet and warm in the kitchen. He looked younger and much less formidable in these surroundings, Anne thought.

"Your bare feet!" she said. "They must be freezing cold on these flags. You should have put some slippers on."

"Yes, Nanny," Robert looked down at his feet and then again at her.

"Is there anything else you want?" Anne asked, turning towards the door. "Would you like some of *Grandma Tyson's* biscuits like James, in case you feel hungry as well as thirsty?"

"I never eat biscuits in bed—not even *Grandma Tyson's*—too many crumbs."

Anne laughed a little forcedly. Why did this man make her feel so shy when he looked at her with those serious grey eyes of his?

She said, "Mother told you I was going to go on working for *Grandma Tyson*. I hope she made it clear that I was to take over her job, be boss as it were of the whole thing. I should have explained this more clearly this morning."

Robert raised his eyebrows at her in surprise and laughed. "My dear girl, I am not going to stand here in my bare feet on these very cold flags, as you chided me, in the middle of the night, and discuss your position at *Grandma Tyson*. Don't worry, there will be plenty of opportunities to discuss your job and your terms of reference—but in your nice comfortable office. Now come back to bed."

Anne flushed a little with embarrassment. She held open the kitchen door for him. "You go first."

"Afraid I might leave the light on?"

"Perhaps. You don't know your way around yet. My mother has economy mania about lights."

She shut the kitchen door and switched on the landing light.

Stealthily, like a couple of conspirators, both of them crept up the stairs.

Robert stood at the bathroom door, ready to fill his glass. "Goodnight, Anne and a thousand more apologies."

Anne went back to her room and climbed into bed. She lay wakeful in the darkness for a long time, thinking about Robert Fordham. Why did she spend so much time thinking about him? Why was he getting under her skin like this, irritating and

177

10

"**D**OES this mean that our marriage is going to be postponed for a year then?" Jack asked.

Anne looked up at him from the plate of canapés she was garnishing. They were in the kitchen and they were alone. It seemed the first time she had been alone with him for days and so she had taken the opportunity to tell him that she had definitely decided to go on working for another year, agreeing to her mother's request. Now, looking at the expression on his face, one of sulky crossness, she wished she had not brought the matter up.

"Not necessarily," she said.

"I can't understand you. You've got this marvellous opportunity to move out. You're going to have enough money to do what you like . . . to tell everyone to go to hell . . . This fellow Fordham is here to take over, your mother is packing it in . . ."

"That's just it," Anne said quickly.

"One of us has got to stay to see the thing through. It's a family business, Jack, and lots of people were worried when they heard about the take-over. I am going to stay and see that everything goes smoothly, to watch out for their interests, as it were. Besides, Robert Fordham has other responsibilities—*Grandma Tyson* is only one of his interests . . . Please understand, Jack," she added a little wistfully.

"I'm sorry, I don't understand—you sound too drearily paternalistic for words —and I don't suppose I ever will understand. It seems to me *Grandma Tyson* comes before everything else in your life . . ."

"Of course, it doesn't," said Anne a little impatiently. She did not know what on earth had possessed her to bring the subject up tonight of all nights. She must be mad.

Barbara Tyson had planned a quiet, intimate family dinner for James and Natalie's first evening with them. Anne had asked if Jack could be included and her mother had agreed, if a little begrudgingly. But Anne, of course, had forgotten about Margot Fratelli. Jack had asked if Margot could come too, since he didn't like leaving her all alone. It had seemed churlish to refuse so now the quiet little family party had been enlarged to include Jack and Margot.

James and Natalie had arrived in the late afternoon and both of them, together with her mother, Margot and Robert, were all enjoying drinks in the sitting-room at this moment.

"Let's just get over the next few weeks," Anne said, "and then we can think about getting married."

"I don't want a working wife," Jack said crossly. "I thought we were going on this tour of the world . . ."

Anne gave him the plate of canapés. "That was just fun and make-believe," she said.

"It wasn't make-believe for me," Jack said, "I meant it seriously. Don't you realise we will be able to do what we like? Go where we want with no brakes? Don't you want to see something of the world?"

"What about your work?" Anne asked. "Surely you want to work too?"

Jack shrugged irritably. "I don't care if I never work again." He went out of the kitchen with the plate. Anne followed him.

Watching Jack pass the canapés round, smiling and joking with their guests, it was difficult to remember how surly he had been a few moments before.

A dreadful, inexorable feeling took possession of Anne's heart. She had made a terrible mistake. She should not have agreed to marry him. It would never work. They would never agree about anything. Maybe she was selfish wanting to go on working for *Grandma Tyson*—but she had obligations too.

It would be much easier to give it all up and go swanning off with Jack—but her conscience would never be quiet if she did such a thing. Surely he could understand that? But he seemed to be making such a dreadful unnecessary fuss about it. It was only a postponement after all.

"Can I recommend these mushroom *vol-au-vents?*" Jack asked Natalie, smiling down at her. Natalie twinkled back up at him, "I picked the mushrooms myself this morning when the dew was still on the grass and the sun just rising, suffusing the skies with an unearthly rosy light."

"I shouldn't think you've ever seen the sun rise in your whole life," Margot interrupted him. "You never get up before twelve." She looked at Natalie. "I warn you. Beware of him. He's a terrible liar."

"I thought you were my friend, Margot," Jack said. "Besides, I have seen the sun rise. Stay up till dawn, that's the answer, don't go to bed at all."

Anne smothered her unwelcome thoughts and went back into the kitchen while the teasing and joshing went on. She had arranged for Maureen to come in later and help with the washing-up, but she was the cook. It had seemed kinder to her mother that she should do the cooking so that Barbara's attention could be devoted entirely to their guests.

Anne was too conscious of her responsibilities as cook to be fully cognisant of everything that was going on, but she was aware that James, seated on Barbara's right, was having long earnest chats with her mother, when he wasn't having to listen to Margot on his other side.

Anne had seated Robert on her right and Natalie was between Robert and Jack. Natalie positively sparkled at both men, but Margot on the other side of the table was well able to capture Robert's attention.

So altogether, on the surface, it seemed a very merry affair, but Anne was glad when everyone agreed they were sated and her mother suggested coffee in the sitting-room. Now she could relax.

Anne went back into the kitchen to get the tray. Maureen had arrived and was already busy at the sink. "You should be wearing a halo," Anne said. She picked up the tray of coffee-cups.

"Let me take that," a voice said. She turned. It was Robert who had followed her.

"It's time you sat down," he said. "A marvellous meal but you've been working too hard, jumping up and down like a yo-yo." Meekly Anne let him take the tray from her. How sweet and thoughtful of him, she thought, but then she supposed he was rather sweet. She had seen that side of him when they first met. She followed him into the sitting-room.

Anne was tired—tired of her thoughts, physically tired by the work she had done. She sat in an easy-chair by the coffee table and poured out the coffees and let the tide of conversation wash over her. They all seemed to be enjoying each other's company very much she thought, listening to both Margot and Natalie chattering away. They were more than a match for each other. She listened, bemused, as her mother's plans for the next day were taken over by Margot and Jack. Between them, they worked out a tour which would take in several lakes and a great deal of the countryside, ending at a fashionable hotel and restaurant at Ullswater.

"I'll book a table in the morning before we set out," Jack said. "It's essential to make reservations."

"Was he going to take them all to lunch?" Anne wondered idly. It was a fearfully expensive place.

Her mother had the same thought. "You can't take us out to lunch," Barbara said. "It'll cost a bomb. Besides . . ."

James interrupted. "Now *I* would like to take you all out to lunch. Do you want to go to this place, Barbara? It seems a long way."

"Of course she does, Pa," said Natalie. "I want to go anyway. It's always being written about. It'll be fun—the food is supposed to be splendid."

James looked across at Barbara for

confirmation. She smiled and shrugged and gave in gracefully. "That's settled then. You're my guests."

"We'll argue about that later," Jack said airily. "Now shall we come and meet here? Or will you pick us up?"

"But I want to show James and Natalie the farm," said Barbara.

"That won't take all morning," Jack answered her.

"I do want to see something of the Lakes while I am here," Natalie put in.

"And so do I," said Margot. "Jack's promised me a tour for ages and done nothing about it."

So the talk went on. Maps were brought out and the route discussed in detail.

"You're very quiet," Robert said at one point to Anne.

"They all seem to know what they want and where they want to go. They don't need any suggestions from me," she answered.

"And yet you know more about the countryside than any of them. You're not always so self-effacing, Anne."

"I guess I'm tired. My batteries need

re-charging and I suppose you're telling me that I'm too pushy."

"I would never use such an unattractive word to describe you, and in any case, it doesn't fit." They were talking quietly under the hubbub of the others' voices.

"What word would you use then?" she asked.

"Now you're looking for compliments—I thought you didn't like them", he said teasingly.

"I never said that. Everyone likes compliments if they're meant."

"I always mean mine. I don't pay them otherwise." He was silent a moment then he added, "I've thought of a word to describe you. Several words—still waters; a deep lake, tranquil under the sky—You can't object to those?"

Before she could answer, his attention was caught by Margot who pulled at his sleeve. "Look at this, Robert. Give this route your approval . . ."

In the end, it seemed settled to everyone's satisfaction, although Anne did not think her mother was best pleased at having the arrangements taken out of her hands by the forceful Margot, with some assistance from Natalie and Jack. But it was difficult for her. She wanted James and Natalie to enjoy themselves.

It was decided that Jack and Margot would come up to Lowater about ten-thirty. "That will give us time to see over the farm," said Natalie. And then they would set out on their journey of exploration, taking two cars.

"The best way to see the country," Anne interrupted at this point, teasingly, "is to walk."

Margot and Natalie looked at her in horror, thinking she meant it. They laughed eventually when they realised she was teasing, but weakly, implying it wasn't a very good joke.

Margot rose from the floor where she had been studying the map. "That's settled then. Now it's time we went home to bed. Come along, Jack darling. I need my beauty sleep if we're going to get up at the crack of dawn."

Jack obediently got up from his chair and followed her out of the room. Anne also rose and went after them. Jack had given her an enigmatic look from his closed-up face as he passed her. She had the strangest feeling that he wanted to go without saying good night to her.

He was still angry with her. Perhaps rightly so; she was too confused to tell. She had thought all her problems would be solved when she had agreed to marry him, but they seemed to have become worse. Perhaps it would have been much fairer to Jack if she had said no; having said yes, she owed him something, and now there was another creeping doubt in her mind. "I don't care if I never work again," he had said, but, of course, he had said it in the heat of the moment. He could not mean it. There were areas in which she and Jack seemed hardly to agree at all. Would it matter? Married couples didn't have to be Siamese twins, after all. To agree all the time would be so boring. Anne resolutely pushed her doubts aside. She reached up to kiss Jack good night. He made the merest of acknowledgements and gave her a quick indifferent kiss on the cheek.

When Jack and Margot had gone, Natalie said to Anne, "I approve of your fiancé, Anne. He's charming." She was standing by Robert's side and she tucked her arm into his and looked up at him. "Isn't he, Robert? Very attractive."

"Very," said Robert, non-commitally. Natalie had made it pretty obvious that she thought Jack attractive, Anne had noted, without animus. All her sparkle had been directed at Jack but Anne felt there was something phoney about it. She had flirted with Jack and kept glancing at Robert to see if he had noticed.

"I can't say I like Margot what's-her-name as much," Natalie went on. She added inquisitively, "What's with her? Is she staying with Jack? Aren't you jealous? I know I should be. She's terribly bossy and possessive."

"She's an old friend," Anne explained. She added a little warily, "I don't think I have anything to be jealous of."

"What are these Gold Leopards she keeps talking about?" asked Robert idly.

"Oh, you are stupid, Robert," said Natalie. "Everyone knows them. They're quite a famous dance troupe. You see them all the time on TV."

"I don't," said Robert.

Natalie might not have liked Margot but Robert seemed to. He had listened to all her hyperbole and preposterous conversation with every appearance of enjoyment. If he wasn't careful, Margot would eat him up, but she supposed wryly that Robert could look after himself.

They had been talking at one end of the sitting-room. Now James and Barbara joined them. It was time for them all to go to bed.

"A lovely evening, my dear," James said to Anne. "What a charming, comfortable house this is!"

It was a long time before Anne got to sleep. Her thoughts milled around in her head like rats in a cage.

She must be honest with herself and look at Jack with unblinkered eyes. He was charming and good-looking and fun to be with, and his love for her had been a kind of intoxication. This was their first real disagreement. Maybe she was silly and juvenile to feel so disillusioned.

She remembered Robert Fordham's words. Marriage was a life sentence. It needn't be, but like him she wanted it to be for keeps once she embarked on it.

Robert Fordham. She was spending too much time thinking about him. Would she think about him quite so much if he were bald, fat and fifty? She guessed that anyone who had been put in Robert's job would have her whole attention. It was inevitable. But Robert was personable and attractive and disturbing. It was difficult to disentangle her interest between the man or the job.

In the morning everyone was up early but James was the earliest of all. He was already outside when Anne was in the kitchen cooking the breakfast. He had found Jimmy Dickson, met some more lambs which had been born during the night and had been having a little inquisitive walk round all by himself.

"But you are not going to do me out of my conducted tour," said Barbara. So after breakfast, he was taken round again. Natalie and Robert and Anne trailed along too, and Barbara showed off her barn and her shippon, and the stables, all white-painted and well-kept but with a certain amount of cosy, inevitable untidiness. They saw the new-born lambs, Natalie cooing over their prettiness and friskiness in the sunshine with their mothers. They saw the bantam hens and the proud and beautiful little bantam cockerel, the guinea fowls and chickens at the bottom of the orchard and the ducklings by the beck.

"What are those black-and-white speckled hens?" asked Natalie.

"They're Marans'," said Barbara, "but I prefer the name an old Scots farmer's wife told me. She called them silver tarr-tan."

"It's like a toy farm," said Natalie. She was as interested as a child and much warmer and more charming than she had been when they first met, Anne thought.

"Yes, I suppose it is," Barbara agreed wistfully. "I suppose I only play at farming, but it pays for itself. We make a profit but it's hard to make a good living out of this much land. We would need more. I don't know what we would have done without *Grandma Tyson* . . . and yet what would this countryside be without its small farms?"

"But you haven't any piglets or cows," said Natalie. "In my toy farm, I always had piglets and cows—"

"I'll see what I can do for your next visit," Barbara smiled. "We sometimes "gist", that is we have other people's cattle

—if we have enough grass, and Jimmy's always on about a pig or two—for our households—but I think he has enough to do. There are the heaf sheep—that is, sheep on the fell—as well as those in the fields. And they've all got to be gathered, and dipped, and shorn at various intervals."

They wandered back to the house, Robert and Anne bringing up the rear.

"Your mother really loves this place, doesn't she?" Robert said. "It'll be hard for her to give it up."

"It's lovely today when the sun's shining," said Anne, "but somehow the rain comes horizontally across the meadow."

"You're not so enamoured?"

She glanced at him quickly, "I love it," she said simply, "Rain or shine."

"You'd find it hard to give up?" He asked the question as though he was deeply interested in her answer.

"I don't think I'm going to be asked to give it up," she said.

"Are you sure of that?"

"If one can be sure of anything," she said lightly.

In the driveway, back at the house,

waiting for them were Margot and Jack. "Come along, come along," cried Margot, "We thought you'd gone without us."

She was looking very smart in a black leather skirt, a bright cerise blouse and a black shawl flung over her shoulders. In her ears swung large turquoise-and-gold earrings.

Anne had put on her best tweed suit this morning. Her jacket and skirt were beautifully cut and very becoming to her slim figure, but in their soft, muted colours made her feel like one of her mother's little hens beside this gypsy flamboyance—and not the silver tarr-tan hens either, she thought ruefully.

The previous night it had been decided that the two cars they would take, for comfort and size, would be Robert's and James's.

Anne was never quite sure how it happened afterwards. The others were in the driveway, Robert went off to get his car from the garages which were a little way from the house; James and Barbara were still walking about the garden. She went inside for a few minutes to pick up her coat and give Maureen a few last-minute instructions. When she went outside again, it was to see the tail of Robert's car going down the drive. Margot was sitting beside him, Jack and Natalie in the back. James and Barbara were standing by James's car.

"Why didn't you go with the others?" Barbara asked, "Margot said you wanted to come with us."

Anne was consumed with a mixture of feelings. Rage was one of them and a dreadful childish feeling of being left out. She wanted to both weep and stamp her foot. Why hadn't Jack waited for her? He had given her a cool but friendly enough greeting this morning, but this was just as horrid as he had been last night.

Pride came to her rescue. She was not going to let her mother see how upset she was.

"I thought I ought to drive," she said gaily, "so that James can look out of the window and you can tell him where he is. That is, if James will trust me to drive his beautiful car."

"I'm sure you are as good a driver as you are a cook," said James gallantly.

"Well, that's very nice and thoughtful of you," said her mother, "and much nicer for James instead of having to keep his eye on the road all the time."

"I suggest you both sit in the back," said Anne firmly, "and I'll be chauffeur." They set off in pursuit of the others.

They did not catch them up. It would be the blind leading the blind, Anne thought. Robert barely knew his way around and Margot, Jack and Natalie would be useless. She hoped, not very charitably, that Margot was a bad map-reader. What had possessed Margot to tell such a lie? Or maybe the information had come from Jack who was still feeling sore and resentful from last night.

The sun shone from a blue sky dappled with unthreatening fleecy little wisps of cloud. The air was fresh and warm. Daffodils and narcissi and blossom were everywhere; the becks and the waterfalls sparkled. Her ill-humour passed away as they drove along. The drive was a particularly beautiful one, giving them glorious and breathtaking vistas of water and mountains. It was good to hear the proprietorial pleasure in her mother's voice as she talked to James.

They arrived at the restaurant at the time

they had planned but there was no sign of the others.

"I expect they got lost," said Barbara philosophically.

Their table, which James had booked that morning, was ready, and they sat down and looked at the elaborate menu. After half-an-hour's waiting, they decided they might as well order and begin their meal.

Their first course had just been served when the others arrived.

Yes, it was true, they had got lost. Margot and Natalie were in giggling form, Robert looked grim and Jack sulky. Robert apologised and they all sat down. James called the waiter and ordered more wine and more menus.

"We had a beautiful drive all the same," said Margot "even if we did go all over the place. I'm not the best map-reader in the world, am I, Robert darling?"

"I should say you're about the worst," Robert said equably, "but there was no one else in the car either who was any better— except of course myself."

"We can't all have a brilliant bump of location," said Jack. He sounded sour and petulant. Something had happened to upset him, or maybe he was just irritable about the delay.

Before leaving, they took a stroll down by the lakeshore. James and Barbara walked in front, Robert, with hobbling Margot on one side hanging on to his arm, Natalie hanging on the other, followed, and Anne and Jack brought up the rear.

Anne dawdled so that the others could go way ahead.

"What's the matter, Jack?" she asked. "Why are you so grumpy?"

"I'm not grumpy."

"You've been grumpy ever since last night. I'm sorry if I've upset you."

"You haven't upset me."

Anne took a deep breath. "I've been thinking things over," she said, "and I think we should finish it. I can't let my mother down and yet if I don't do what you want, I feel I am letting you down. There seems no point in our going on like this."

"I thought we were in love," said Jack, his calm face registering no feeling. He stooped down and picked up a flat stone and sent it skimming across the water.

"So did I."

"We have one little disagreement and you want to break it off."

"It isn't a little disagreement."

"I don't want to finish it," said Jack softly. "I don't think you do really. You're threatening me because I won't agree to what you want to do."

"You make me sound unreasonable."

"Aren't you?"

"I don't think its unreasonable to want to go on working for *Grandma Tyson* for just another year. We would have all the time in the world afterwards to go on your tour. It's only a postponement."

"I wonder," said Jack. "At the end of the year, something else will crop up and you'll still want to trundle along in the same old humdrum way in this humdrum backwater. I want some excitement in my life."

"I'm sorry you think I'm humdrum."

"Oh, don't be so idiotic. I don't think you're humdrum. Only your ideas. I'm not going to let you go, Anne."

Anne fell silent. It was difficult to describe her feelings. Such a mixture of sadness and disillusion and regret. "I just feel it wouldn't work."

"My darling girl, you really are talking the most absolute rubbish. So, okay, I don't like the thought of being stuck here for another year, but I guess I'll survive. You can go on being the busy little working woman and I'll just be the house-husband."

"That's just it," Anne wanted to say, "I don't want a house-husband."

"Give me another chance," Jack said. He put his arm round her shoulder. "Please, darling, we can't let one little spat foul things up. We've got too much going for us."

"But it's more fundamental than that," Anne said.

"Is it? I don't think so." He pulled her round to face him and kissed her, holding her tight, but after a while, he sensed the old magic was not there and held her away from him and looked into her face.

"You can't leave me now, Anne," he said. "It would break my heart." His expression was sad. "You can't know what you've meant to me these past few months —a new life almost—new hopes, new horizons . . . don't cast me down into the depths again . . . you're not going to, are you?"

"No," Anne said unwillingly.

"Come on," he took hold of her hand, "we're getting left behind," and hand-in-hand they ran after the others and caught them up.

There was some suggestion they should switch passengers for the drive back.

"Oh, we're all right as we are," Anne said, her cheerful tones belying her drooping spirits, "You can all get lost again. It won't matter on the way back."

"I almost forgot," said Jack, "I've got an invitation for all of you for this evening at the Brackens'. George is barbecuing . . . he started this morning before we left . . . and he and Myra would like you all to come."

"What fun!" cried Natalie.

"There'll be a few others coming," said Jack. "We thought we'd have it in my barn —there's more room—and maybe bop a little—to records. Sorry, Natalie, we can't produce a real live group."

"Sounds very nice," said Barbara faintly. On the way home, she was more forceful. "None of my plans for this weekend are going right," she said. "Do you really want to go to this barbecue, James?"

"Do you?"

"It's not really my idea of fun, sitting on the floor of a barn with a plate of half-cooked meat on my lap and sloppy salad sliding all over the place, and nowhere to put your drink . . ." began Barbara.

"It's not mine either," said James. "Why don't we let the youngsters go to the barbecue and you and I find ourselves a nice little pub somewhere?"

"Or we could stay home."

They argued amicably for a few moments, and then decided to leave it until later to see how they felt at the end of the day.

Anne thought, "I am stuck with the barbecue." She was quite sure the meat would not be half-cooked. If George had anything to do with it, everything would be beautifully prepared and delicious, but somehow she knew she was not going to enjoy her evening.

The barbecued sheep was ambrosial. George had secured two carcases to two metal rods and hung them on a metal rack over a deep pit of charcoal embers. The meat had been cooking slowly all day, basted at frequent intervals by George from a great dish of herby marinade, heavily spiked with wine. Myra had made several salads, all arranged in large wooden bowls. There were baked potatoes, home-made breads, and a lot of Italian plonk, as well as home-made elderflower and parsnip wine. There was a large wooden platter of assorted cheeses (including goats-milk made by Myra from the nanny they kept). There were fruit pies—apple, blackcurrant, cherry out of the freezer— and huge jugs of cream, and of course yoghurt (the proper Balkan kind, self-perpetuating).

The dividing screens in Jack's barn had been moved and set along the whitewashed walls, which had been further hung with shawls and huge abstract paintings done by Myra and George. One end had been cleared for dancing, the other strewn with rugs and cushions, sag-bags, benches, garden-chairs, an assortment of seating. Lighting was soft and indirect—candles, large and small, stuck in bottles. The stereo was turned up to its fullest volume.

The great barn was shadowy and

mysterious and reverberated with sound. About one hundred people had been invited and there was quite a crush. It was too cold to stay long outside round the barbecue which had been built some way from the house and barn. George sat patiently near his fire, enveloped in a sheepskin coat. Once he sat there with an umbrella over his head during a shower of rain, but finally the meat was done and was brought inside on a wooden table-top to great acclaim.

Robert had driven Natalie and Anne over to Cragfall. "What will you wear?" Natalie had asked Anne. "Jeans, trousers, something comfortable," Anne had suggested, "and take a cardigan or stole. The barn will be pretty draughty." But surprisingly, with the crowd of people, plus the fact that Myra had installed a couple of electric radiators at each end, it wasn't.

They were greeted by Myra in the doorway with Jack at her side, holding a tray of filled wine glasses. "You must look after yourselves," Myra cried. "The bar's on the left, food on the right."

"Red or white?" asked Jack. "Home made plonk or Italian plonk?"

Among the shadows and the crowd of people, Anne lost Robert and Natalie almost immediately. She took a drink from Jack and saw that he was too busy as host to bother much with her. He had greeted her with all his old exuberance, giving her a smacking kiss, much to the danger of the tray of glasses.

The crowd of guests were the Brackens' usual disparate mixture—off-comers like themselves who wrote or painted or potted or practised other arts and crafts, skilfully or badly; people who worked in Athelstone or Hunthorpe at more prosaic labours in the chemical and engineering plants; the local schoolmaster, plus wife; the local doctor plus wife; farming and landed neighbours. It was a curiously assorted mishmash of people. In the years the Brackens had lived there, they had made many friends, their taste was catholic and they had no inhibitions about mixing different groups.

Anne knew most of them and there were plenty of people to engage her attention.

She heard the noise when the meat was brought in and saw Jack help George put it on the trestle table at one side of the room. It was time to eat and the guests began to move forward, but it was some time before Anne found herself in the queue at the table. As she had threaded her way there, she had been stopped by people she knew.

As she helped herself to food, she felt a hand on her arm. She turned to find Robert at her elbow. "I've been looking all over for you," he said. "What a mob! I'm getting some food for Margot."

He waited until she had helped herself and then steered her through the crowd to the far end of the room. Here, sitting among cushions and rugs, like Scheherezade in the *Arabian Nights*, was Margot.

She did not look too pleased to see Anne, but made a space among the cushions and Anne and Robert sat down, Anne cross-legged so that she could manage her plate better. She could feel Robert staring at her. "How very supple you are," he said, "You must be double jointed."

"I can't sit properly because of my ankle," Margot said, "and I can't dance!" She sounded irritable. "I didn't know there were going to be so many people. Myra and George have been buzzing round like a couple of lunatics. I couldn't help at all because of my ankle—and all my clothes and belongings have been moved. I couldn't find a thing." She sounded very aggrieved. "How long will it go on? Do you realise I won't be able to go to bed until everyone has gone? It might not be for hours!"

"What have you done with Natalie?" Anne asked Robert, more to change the subject than because she wanted to know.

Margot answered for him. "Oh, Natalie's all right. Your everloving fiancé is looking after her. I saw them dancing."

Anne looked down at her food and tried to ignore the spite. She felt very much a gooseberry sitting there with them. Obviously Margot wished her a million miles away.

"Jack's looking after everyone, and the bar," Robert said.

His words did not make Anne feel any better. She didn't want to be pitied for Jack's seeming lack of attention.

Margot talked on, raising her voice against the music. "I really don't know why the Brackens had to ask so many people. Who on earth are they?"

"Friends and neighbours," Anne said.

"Do you know them?"

"Most of them."

At the far end in the dim, shadowed depths of the barn, Anne could see the gyrating figures of the dancers. The music was enticing, had gentled to a low throbbing. She tapped her foot in time.

As though he read her mind, Robert asked softly, "Would you like to dance?"

"You can't leave me all alone," Margot said, "I don't know a soul."

"That's easily remedied," said Anne, nettled. She suddenly felt mad at Margot's petulance and self absorption. She rose to her feet. She looked around her and saw David Satterthwaite, whom she'd known since they were at playschool together, wandering by with a plate of food in one hand, a glass in the other, obviously looking for a place to sit.

"Hi, David," she said. "Come and join us!"

David turned gratefully and sank among the cushions. He called to a chum who had been close behind him. "Come here, Tom! Here's some room!"

Anne introduced the newcomers to Margot and Robert. She looked then at Robert, and he got to his feet and followed her to the other end of the room where the dancers were.

"You don't have to dance with me," Anne said contrarily.

"You made it pretty obvious you wanted to," he said. "Anything to oblige a lady."

When they reached the dance floor, the music suddenly came to an abrupt end.

"That's that then," said Anne, and turned away.

Robert put out a restraining hand. "They're only changing cassettes," he said.

In a few moments, more music seeped into the air. This time it was in a different tempo, a slow, schmaltzy old tune, *Begin the Beguine*.

Robert put his hands on either side of her waist and swayed in time with her, hardly moving, looking down at her intently.

"Funny, unpredictable Anne," he said softly, "What a mass of contradictions you are. So calm, so self possessed, so assured, so beautiful; and yet you let your happiness depend on that—that lemon!"

Startled, Anne looked up to meet his gaze.

"Lemon?"

"I mean Jack—spring-heeled Jack, lightweight Jack."

"You've been talking to my mother."

"I've been talking to no one. I've just been using my eyes. You're not in love with him, Anne, don't kid yourself."

"You say that because you think he's not in love with me."

"I do not. He's in love with you all right. It would not be difficult to be in love with you. He's in a temper with you now because you won't do what he wants—"

"Who told you that?"

"No one has told me anything. The onlooker sees most of the game, you know. He's a lightweight, Anne, not worthy of you."

"Now I know you've been talking to my mother. She says that all the time. At least she knows me. You do not. I have been in love with Jack for a very long time—"

"And you're not going to admit you're not for anyone. One of these days, you'll

211

really fall in love and wonder what hit you. Do you remember our talk that lunch-time —it seems a year, but it was not so long ago?"

"Vaguely," lied Anne. "And I told you too much about myself," she thought.

"I'll remind you. We talked of love. Shall I tell you what's going to happen with Jack? You're going to boss the hell out of him. He won't be able to stand up to you. He'll do whatever you say in the end and in the end you'll despise him for his weakness."

"I can't bear amateur psychologists. You make me sound charming."

"Yes, you are charming, and completely wasted on Jack."

She felt the pressure of his hands on her waist. Her own hands had been resting on his arms. Now almost involuntarily she raised them and linked them behind his neck, and they stayed like that for some minutes, moving gently to the sensuous beat. It was as though they were suspended in time, with no thought, only sensation, lapped by the music. Desire crept through her veins like a slow, not-to-be-gainsaid tide. She wondered what it would be like to kiss him and was angry that such an idea should even enter her head. The music whispered to an end, there was a pause, and the spell was broken. They stared at each other like people who have come out of a dream, still holding one another.

This was obviously a cassette of oldies. Another one came on the air sung by Peggy Lee: *"The Man I love . . ."*

"How very suitable," said Robert.

"He'll come along . . . And he'll be big and strong . . ." the crooner sang throatily *". . . The Man I love . . ."*

"How very unsuitable!" said Robert.

Anne tried to disentangle herself from his encircling arms.

But he held her fast. "Tonight you're not getting away from me," he said. Anne gave in, and gave in too to the pleasure of moving with him to the gentle, insistent rhythm. He held her close and they danced to the end of the cassette. The tempo changed and became fast and furious and the sound reached a new high. Anne flung herself away from him, and bopped by herself, whirling herself about in abandon, trying to lose all thoughts and feelings in the dance. He was there with her, digging into the deck, his eyes watching her, his hand catching hers occasionally to spin her round. It ended and, a little breathless and brought back to earth, Anne walked away. He followed her and put his hand on her waist to guide her back to the shadows at the end of the barn where Margot was sitting.

She had discovered something about herself she did not like and could not understand. She was deeply attracted to Robert Fordham. His touch had the power to move her. She had wanted to go on dancing held in his arms for ever. She was crazy.

They found Margot holding court, with several men in attendance. Her irritation at the barbecue seemed to have disappeared.

Robert flopped down on the chair beside her and put out his hand to Anne. "Come and sit down."

"No, I have a headache," she said. "I want to go home but I don't want to spoil your evening . . . and Natalie's . . . I'll borrow Jack's car. Don't worry about me."

Before he could say anything more to detain her, she had fled into the crowd.

She could not find Jack anywhere but she found George resting from his labours by the table and having another slice of his delicious meat. "Would you tell Jack I'm borrowing his car as I want to go home? I've got a terrible headache," and indeed by now this was not a lie. "It's been a marvellous party. I'll ring Myra in the morning. So kind of you to include us all." She ran down the barn steps as though the Furies were after her. She found Jack's car and drove out of the yard, steering a careful if erratic way between the other cars which were parked all over the place.

When she arrived home it was to find Lowater all in darkness. Her mother and James had not yet returned, or else had gone to bed. She looked at her watch. Eleven-thirty. It wasn't very late so possibly they were still out. The dogs gave her a vociferous welcome, and after greeting them, she went straight upstairs to bed.

She lay wakeful for a long time, staring into the darkness. She heard her mother and James come home, several hours later. She heard Natalie and Robert return. She heard the grandfather clock strike three.

Why should she mind what Robert Fordham said about Jack? He didn't know him. Why should it bother her? Why should he get under her skin like this? But she knew it did bother her. Even more than that, she was bothered by the sensation which had taken possession of her while they were dancing. What was the matter with her, losing her cool like this? How dare Robert call Jack a lemon and a lightweight?

Nobody liked hearing home truths. It had been her fault that she and Jack had had their disagreement. Was she demanding too much, insisting on working for another year? She had never even thought Jack was serious about his fantasies of a world tour. What would they use for money, for a start? Her mother's? It would cost a fortune. Money never seemed to come into it. But it would have to eventually.

But this morning, Jack had given in to her wishes. Not very agreeably perhaps. What had he said—he hadn't liked the thought of "being stuck here for another year." Those words had cut her to the heart. As though being here was purgatory. But here was her home. This place she loved. She did not want to swan off into the wild blue yonder now—or even in a year's time.

She remembered what Robert had said —"You're going to boss the hell out of him. He won't be able to stand up to you. He'll do whatever you say in the end and in the end you'll despise him for his weakness."

Jack was not as weak as all that, but she knew now she could not marry him. Their differences were too fundamental. She had made a mistake. Her mother had been right. And Robert Fordham—however hard the admission—was right too. Robert Fordham—ah, there was another problem. Was she falling in love with the man? What sort of fickle creature did that make her? Engaged to one man, falling in love with another. Was it love, this extraordinary yearning she had for Robert—for his whole attention and regard? She knew from tonight that he found her attractive, but then he found Margot attractive too.

If Margot had been able to dance, perhaps he would have taken no notice of herself. Tonight had perhaps been just another evening's entertainment for him. For her, it had been a cataclysmic tunnelling into her utmost being. Her feelings for Jack had paled into dim insignificance beside the storm of longing which had taken possession of her.

11

AT breakfast next morning, Natalie said politely, "I hope your headache's better. Robert said you felt unwell last night."

"I was just tired, I guess," Anne said, "and I found the music rather loud."

"Marvellous party!" said Natalie. "I had a wonderful time, danced off both my shoes. Jack's got a lovely plan for us all today."

"Jack can keep his lovely plan," said Barbara Tyson quickly. "I have a lovely plan for us all too. This weekend is getting out of hand."

"And what is your lovely plan, my dear?" asked James.

"That you and I go for a walk and that you let me show you our beautiful tarn up in the fells behind the house. That we then come home and eat a delicious piece of roast lamb, and read the Sunday papers."

"I agree, that's a lovely plan," said James.

Natalie pulled a face. "Jack said he'd take us fishing."

"I'm going to cook the lunch," said Anne.

"And I'm going to help you," said Robert.

"Do you mean I've got to go fishing on my own?"

"I expect Margot will go too," said Barbara kindly. Natalie looked at Robert persuasively. He shook his head at her. "We can't leave Anne all on her own slaving away over a hot stove."

"I shall be perfectly all right," said Anne. "I've only got to stick the meat in the oven."

"I'm not in the mood for fishing," said Robert.

So in the end Natalie went off on her own, looking rather forlorn in a waterproof jacket, several sizes too large for her, borrowed from Anne.

James and Barbara set off on their walk, and Robert followed Anne into the kitchen after waving them goodbye.

"I can manage by myself," Anne said. "There's very little to do." He seemed large and overpowering. He took away her deftness and skill.

"You're not going to get rid of me," he said, "I am determined to be useful. Shall I make the mint sauce? I'm very good at mint sauce—*cordon bleu* standard."

"We're having redcurrant jelly."

"Oh, can't we have mint sauce as well? Please! I'm very fond of mint sauce. So's James."

Silently, refusing to smile at his jokiness, she gave him the vinegar from a shelf in the cupboard above her head, and told him where to find some mint growing at the back of the house near the kitchen door. She began scraping the new potatoes.

He came back with a great bunch of mint, washed it and started chopping. "You're feeling better this morning?"

"Of course. I was just tired."

"You don't have to worry, you know."

"Worry?"

"I got the message when you ran away from me last night. You're safe from my advances. I won't take advantage of any momentary lapse on your part but my, my, you can cut a mean rug."

"A mean rug?"

"One of my nasty Americanisms. Did I ever tell you I spent a year in the US after leaving university? It had a bad effect on me. No, of course, I haven't told you. There are a lot of things I haven't told you about myself. We still have a lot to learn about each other. I mean you can dance, dear girl. You're angry with me?"

"Of course I'm not. Why should I be?"

"For daring to criticise the charming Jack."

She put the potatoes on one side and turned to look at him. There was a lovely scent of chopped mint in the air. He met her glance and for a moment she felt she was spinning out of control. "I don't give a damn for your criticism," she said. "It doesn't matter to me what you think of Jack—or of me, for that matter."

"Methinks the lady doth protest too much," he said with mock solemnity. "Anyway, that's a load off my mind. I shall now declare open season on Jack and feel free to criticise, poke fun, or otherwise undermine him at every opportunity."

"But why?" she asked. "How hurtful of you." He had so much more power and authority than Jack would ever have.

"A good question," he said, "and one I've asked myself. And answered. I can't bear waste—and I can't bear to think of Jack unhappy—and married to you," he added with a laugh.

"Oh, you!" She felt like throwing the basin of potatoes at him, water and all, but she didn't. She began scraping again.

"That's not my head," he said looking at her. "There won't be any potato left if you attack it like that. Here, let me do them." He took the knife away from her and moved the bowl of potatoes. "No, you're right. I do not really care about Jack's happiness. I care more about yours."

She wished she could believe him. "I can look after my own happiness, thank you," she said, but she wondered forlornly if she could. "Why should you worry about it?"

"Why indeed?" He stared intently down at the potatoes. "Because I'm a lunatic, I suppose, busy digging a hole for myself. Or perhaps I don't want my managing director to be distracted from her work. Except by me," he added and looked at her, a glint in his eye.

"Jack has never distracted me from my work," she said. That was, after all, part of the trouble but she was not going to admit it to him.

She longed to stand close to him, to lean against him as though he were something solid like a tree, to break the tension which had suddenly grown up between them. If he made a move towards her, she knew she would fall into his arms and weakly let him kiss her if he wanted. He would know then how vulnerable she was and how idiotic.

"These are finished," he said. "Where's the saucepan for them?" She took one down off its hook on the kitchen wall and he gave her the potatoes. She took a sprig of mint from the heap he had not chopped up and put it in with the potatoes.

He turned back to his chopping-board. She gave him a jug and some brown sugar and he scooped up the heap of dark green, chopped mint and put it in the jug. She felt she was engaged in some kind of crazy waltz, moving round him as though terrified of bumping into him.

He stirred his mixture of mint, sugar and vinegar with concentration for a few seconds and set it aside.

He turned away from her restlessly. "Now give me something else to do. Shall

I lay the table? Where are the knives and forks?"

The moment of danger, of truth had passed. Anne took a deep breath as though she had been running.

"I'll show you," she said, walking into the dining-room.

He set the table with her and afterwards went and busied himself with the newspapers until the others returned.

12

EARLY on Monday morning James and Robert and Barbara went off to *Grandma Tyson's*. This was strictly business. James was going to be shown over the factory. Natalie stayed behind and Anne politely stayed with her to give her breakfast.

Natalie was slow in getting up but she eventually appeared, as pretty as ever in her travelling clothes, skin-tight jeans and a sloppy-joe sweater which made her look even more petite and fragile.

"Don't let me forget my trout," she said, nibbling at a piece of toast. Natalie had proudly returned the previous evening with two fish she had caught.

"I've wrapped them in foil and packed them in ice," said Anne, "so they should last the journey."

"Jack was going to eat his for breakfast," said Natalie, "but, ugh! I can't face anything at breakfast except toast and coffee. Have you known Jack long?"

"Long enough."

"He's had an exciting life, hasn't he? But I suppose newspapermen always do. You're going on a safari round the world, he told me. I must say I envy you. I've always wanted to travel."

"But you have travelled."

"Oh, Europe," she discounted. "Looking at all those boring cathedrals in Italy, and finishing school in Paris, and skiing in Switzerland . . . of course there was New York too but I don't call that travel. I'd like to go on safari and sail in a junk and go up the Amazon in Brazil . . ."

"Maybe you will one day." Evidently Jack had been spinning his enticing yarns and here they had taken hold. His audience had been receptive.

"I might, I suppose. But I don't want to go in a pack of people, all milling and moiling in and out of planes and trains. I'd like to go with someone I love, just the two of us, wandering round the world, seeing strange sights and strange exotic people. Jack tells me he will write a book about your travels."

"Well, he is a writer, you know, so I suppose it's natural."

Natalie looked at her watch. "How long is the parent going to be, d'you suppose? Looking at this boring old factory? Oops, sorry! I forgot it was yours. I've waited so often for Pa as he's trailed round some gloomy, derelict old ruin, thinking of taking it over."

As she spoke, they heard the sound of a car. James and Barbara had returned home.

They hurried into the house, smiling and laughing, full, it seemed to Anne, of a barely-suppressed excitement. Obviously, the tour round *Grandma Tyson* had been a great success.

"We're off," said James. "Are you ready, Natalie?"

"My case is packed—upstairs," said Natalie. "My trout!" But Anne had already remembered and brought them out of the fridge for her.

Having waved them off and seen the car disappear down the drive, Anne and Barbara walked back into the house. Barbara caught hold of Anne's hand.

"I've got something to tell you," she said leading the way into the sitting-room. She turned to face her daughter, "I've told James I'll marry him."

"Oh, Mother darling!" Anne gave her mother a big spontaneous hug. "I thought —no, I knew—there was something in the wind. When did he ask you?"

"Some time ago," Barbara admitted. "Not long after I met him—but I wanted time to think—about you—and the business—and then when I knew for sure you were going to stay on for another year . . . It wasn't only that, of course . . . I became more certain in my mind. He is a lovely man, don't you think? But that house it's all rather overpowering . . . I don't know how I'll cope . . ."

"You'll cope beautifully. I know my Mamma," said Anne with conviction. "I'm so happy for you. I like James very much indeed . . ."

"I can't believe my feelings," Barbara said. "Widowed for twenty years—I never thought to feel like this about a man again . . . The weekend went off well, didn't it?" She walked about the room, touching various objects in it, moving an ash-tray, re-aligning a photograph, pulling at an arrangement of flowers. She was nervous and excited.

"The weekend went beautifully," said

Anne. "They both seemed to enjoy themselves very much. And what about *Grandma Tyson*? Did James approve of the set-up?"

"Oh, yes," said Barbara vaguely. "But he depends a lot on Robert, you know, and his judgement."

"When are you going to get married?" Anne asked.

"We haven't decided that yet. Soon, I expect. At our age, what is the point of waiting? You don't mind, Anne?"

"I'm happy for you," Anne said softly. "And so will Sarah and Jenny be when they know. You deserve a lovely life after all the hard work."

"I shall miss all this." Her mother threw out an encompassing arm. "But James loved the place too. He thought it was so wonderfully peaceful and calm. He said we could—and would—come here a lot . . . It was so beautiful up at the tarn yesterday—nobody there but us and the water as still as a mirror and the curlews crying . . . it was lovely . . . it was so marvellous for me that James liked it so much. And Natalie liked it too. That was important. His daughter is very dear to him . . . as my daughters are to me. I couldn't have borne it if you hadn't liked James. Jenny and Sarah seemed to like him too when they met him in London. In fact, I don't think I could agree to marry him unless you approved."

"Oh, Mother darling!" Anne protested.

"It's true," Barbara said. She sat down suddenly. "Now, Anne, what are your plans?"

"They're the same. I shall stay on for another year, as I promised."

"And marriage? What about that?"

"Oh, we'll wait. Don't fuss. Later perhaps," said Anne evasively. She must, for Jack's sake, make a clean break with him before she told her mother.

"James wants to take a long honeymoon," Barbara said. "There are all sorts of places he wants to show me . . ."

"Where will you be married?" asked Anne.

"Maybe quietly in London—perhaps with a big party at an hotel afterwards . . . we only discussed it very briefly . . . Oh, Anne darling, I feel so excited I don't know what to do with myself. I think I'll go for a long walk."

"And I shall take myself off to Athelstone," Anne said. The weekend weather had broken and she drove in a shower of soft spring rain into the town, her mind and brain busy with the implications of her mother's news.

Her mother was going to go away. No wonder she had been so anxious for Anne to stay on. Her mother was going to have a wonderful life. She would be more than capable of running that beautiful house and a London flat, especially with all the help with which James had surrounded himself. Her mother deserved all the luxury and she would appreciate it. But of course it would be a wrench for her to leave Lowater and all her friends. And she would miss *Grandma Tyson*, however much she told herself she was tired of working.

Anne arrived at her office to be greeted by Beryl. Beryl would be one of the people she'd miss.

"Mr. Fordham is in his office and would like to see you as soon as you get in," Beryl said.

Anne checked her mail and then went in to see Robert.

He was brisk and business-like. The

teasing man of the weekend had gone and here was the workaday Robert, wasting no time.

"James get off all right?" he asked perfunctorily, and then turned to a note-pad on his desk. "I've got a few queries here and also some things I'd like to mention."

He ran down the list and she was able to answer most of his questions off the top of her head. The few that she couldn't she promised to look into. At length, he said, "The final thing—I've got a time and motion study team coming down to see me at Hunthorpe so I thought they could have a look round here, too. Could you give me a date when it would be convenient?"

"Time and motion study?"

"We always do it. I expect even in your efficient little operation, there'll be some corners we can cut."

"How do they work?"

He looked a little surprised at her question. "Well, there are three of them and they make a plan of all the operations and break them down and see if they can't be done a little better—or quicker—or cheaper—or whatever."

"Any time would be convenient, I suppose," said Anne doubtfully.

"Good, I'll arrange for them to come some time in the next few weeks, and perhaps you would alert Beryl to find some accommodation for them—in a pub, or local boarding house or something comfortable."

"Is that all?" asked Anne formally. She was irritated by this curt, laconic Robert. Had she ever danced with this man to *Begin the Beguine*? Had he ever said he cared about her happiness?

"Isn't it enough?" he asked. Before she could answer the door of his office burst open and Margot Fratelli erupted into the room, much to their great mutual surprise.

"Of course he'll see me!" Margot was saying to the agitated figure of Beryl close behind her. "I'm his dearest friend!"

"Oh, Mr. Fordham—" Beryl said.

"It's quite all right, Beryl," Robert said. He looked at Margot and drew out a chair for her.

In her hand, Margot had a sheaf of papers. These she now threw on the desk.

"Orders to view," she said. "There are about ten million houses and cottages to

234

rent around here but I have picked out the best ones. I thought we could go and look at them this afternoon."

"Oh, Margot!" said Robert helplessly.

"Well, you said you wanted to move as soon as possible so I trotted round to all the estate agents this morning—and there are masses of things to let. Of course, all the rents go up in the holiday season, but if you take something for a year, they even the rent out so it's not so bad . . ."

"Hold your horses!" Robert held up a hand. He looked across at Anne. "There's no hurry, is there?"

"You can stay with us as long as you like. I'm sure my mother made that clear," she said politely, "But, of course, if you want to find a place of your own . . ."

"He told me he did. I thought there *was* a hurry," said Margot a little truculently.

"I can't impose on your hospitality for ever," Robert said to Anne, "but I didn't mean to make it sound quite so urgent."

Margot picked up the top sheet of the orders to view: "*Charming seventeenth century cottage,*" she read, "*flagged floors, wealth of old beams, modern bathroom and kitchen.*"

Robert took the sheet from her and collected up the sheaf of papers. "I'll read them all this evening. I can't look at anything today, Margot."

"Shall I look at them for you? I could weed them out as it were?"

Anne rose to her feet. "I'll leave you two to sort it out. Just let me know when you're leaving, Robert," she added sweetly.

She laughed a little to herself at his discomfiture when she got back to her own office, but there was a certain wryness about her amusement. Had he been so uncomfortable with them at Lowater that he had to move out in such a rush?

Beryl came in with a cup of coffee for her. "Who was that extraordinary girl?" she asked. "She pushed right past me when I asked her what she wanted. If she's one of Mr. Fordham's friends, I don't think much of his choice."

"I think she's trying to be helpful, and she's probably bored," said Anne charitably. "He's staying with us as you know, and she wants to help him find somewhere else."

"Your mother's just phoned," said Beryl. "Isn't it lovely news! Although I guessed. I could tell from the way she talked about Mr. Millard. Something came into her voice and eyes."

"You're an old romantic," said Anne fondly. "Yes, it is good news."

"We'll miss her," said Beryl, "but, you know, I've got used to the thought of her retiring—and we've still got you."

She looked up at the blown-up old sepia photograph of Grandma Tyson which decorated Anne's wall. "There'll still be a Tyson here," she said to it. "That should please you, old girl."

Anne looked up at Grandma Tyson. She was rather a severe-looking woman, dressed in an opulent silk, black dress with a white lace collar secured at her throat with a large cameo brooch. Her hair was scraped back from her face and on top was a little white lace cap. She sat very upright in a high-backed chair, her hands folded neatly in her lap. Beside her was a round table covered with a bobble-fringed cloth. On the table was a thick-leaved plant and a book, probably the Good Book itself.

It was easy to imagine wise Cumbrian sayings coming out of that firm mouth. "There's nowt so queer as folk" and

"Never say dee sae lang as ye can see owt trailin' aboot".

"I think she'd be hard to please," she said, "but maybe she'd like James."

Margot popped her head round the door.

"I'm off," she said. "I've just got a wigging from Robert for jumping the gun. I hope I didn't upset you but he did tell me he wanted to move out as soon as possible. Being a guest does cramp one's style a bit, doesn't it? After all, you can't treat someone's home like an hotel, can you? I'm off now to case the joints and see if there's one suitable for his lordship. See you!"

She shut the door, quite sure, Anne thought, that by her apology she had put matters right. Instead, she had made matters worse if Anne judged by her feeling of mortification. All the time he had been so pleasant and charming to her mother and so admiring, he had wanted to get away as fast as he could.

Beryl heard her buzzer and left to answer it. A short while afterwards Robert himself appeared in her office.

"Anne, I'm sorry if Margot gave you the wrong impression. You and your mother have been so very kind I would hate you to think . . ."

"Oh, please, don't give it another thought. We've loved having you but, of course, you must find somewhere of your own if you are going to stay up here any length of time."

"You're offended."

"Of course I'm not," she said sharply. "Don't let us make a production of it."

"Okay." He stared at her for a long moment, seemed to be about to say something, decided against it, and stayed silent.

"Just as a matter of curiosity, how long *are* you staying up here?" Anne asked.

"Are you interested?"

"Naturally, I would like to know."

"It depends. The development at Hunthorpe—building the new factory and refurbishing the old—could take a year or two. So I'll be around for a while yet to get in your hair." He paused and smiled, taking the sting out of the words. "But, of course, I will go back to London fairly often. That's why it seemed a good idea to get a place of my own. I can come and go without feeling either a nuisance or ill-mannered."

"You don't have to explain," Anne said.

13

OF course, it was inevitable that Anne should hear more about Robert's search for accommodation.

Margot was there at Cragfall when she went to see Jack after work. She had spent all day as far as Anne could gather looking at cottages and places to rent, and was full of their varied charms and horrors.

"I've made a short list," she said. "Robert is coming round later for supper. He can decide then which ones he wants to see. I know which one I would like."

The barn was now back to its normal state with its screens in position. The table in the dining area was already set for two with knives and forks, wine-glasses and napkins in place.

"What are you giving Robert to eat?" asked Jack.

"I've made a great big beef stew, and I thought we'd have noodles, and Myra has given us some of the cheese she had left over from Saturday . . ."

"There's enough for us then," said Jack. "I think we'll join you, Margot. It's time you returned some of Anne's hospitality. What do you say, Anne?"

"If Margot thinks there'll be enough . . . we don't want to spoil her arrangements," said Anne doubtfully.

Margot did not answer for a moment, then manners prevailed and she said, "I suppose there'll be enough."

"Good," said Jack. He was sitting on the sofa beside Anne and he picked up her hand nearest to him and idly played with her fingers. He had phoned her during the day and had been his old cheerful self. He had noticed nothing amiss with her cautious, guarded replies to his high spirits. Sometime soon she had to talk to him, to persuade him that it really was finished between them. It was not going to be easy. She didn't want to hurt him. She didn't want to cast him down in the depths again as he had described.

Margot switched on the stereo and then busied herself with the table, laying two more places, putting more plates to warm in the oven. Jack and Anne stayed silent on the sofa still holding hands. Anne felt too tired to offer help and Jack seemed under no obligation.

They were still like this, tranquilly listening to the music when Robert arrived.

His eyes flickered over them with hostility. Maybe he was miffed that he wasn't to have a nice *tête à tête* dinner with Margot, Anne thought.

"Now, Robert, you shall hear all about my day," Margot cried when she saw him. She reached up and gave him a hug and a big smacking kiss on the lips. "I've been very busy on your behalf. I've looked at hundreds, no thousands of places, some of them awful beyond words, full of plastic tables, and others as dreamy as a midsummer night."

She began scuffling among her various papers and brought out a very large note-book, the pages of which were covered in her very large handwriting.

"Now here's a cottage in Bosthwaite . . ."

"Where's that?" asked Robert.

"About twenty miles from here," supplied Anne.

"Too far," said Robert.

"Oh, but it's charming, so pretty, the garden full of daffodils and there's a dear old soul next door who'll provide you with meals and clean for you, just like Mrs. Tiggy Winkle or maybe Beatrix Potter herself."

"Beatrix Potter was quite fierce," said Anne. "I don't think she'd have cleaned for anyone, except maybe Herdwick sheep."

"It's still too far."

"Okay—well then, here's another place. This is an old barn which has been converted into two units . . ."

"Where is it?"

Margot studied her notes—"Dodgebarrow."

Robert looked at Anne.

"Quite a reasonable distance," she said. "What's the name of the place? I may know the people." She did, and agreed it might be a possible.

"Then there's this place," said Margot. "It's the wing of an old house overlooking the water. It's rather sparsely furnished but that wouldn't matter, would it? Because you can put a few of your own things in."

"Where is it?"

"It's on the water, and you would

have your own landing-stage. It's called Rawlinson Ground . . ."

"Oh, I know it," said Anne. "I knew the old man who lived there."

"There's no one living there now," said Margot, "except an odd-job-man, a rather grumpy old chap. You would have part of the house, own separate entrance, two bedrooms, one big living-room."

"Old Mr. Collins died a few years back," said Anne, "and the place has been empty ever since. Isn't it rather shabby and neglected? I believe a nephew inherited and didn't know what to do with it."

"Well, he does now," said Margot. "He's turning the place into holiday flats, and this is one of them. It's full of the most wonderful atmosphere—and then there's the water. We could have the most lovely picnics . . . there's a little island on the lake . . ."

"Okay, I'll look at that one, and one or two of the others. Give me the particulars, Margot, and I'll get Beryl to make appointments for me tomorrow."

"I'll do that for you," said Margot eagerly, "and I'll come and look at them with you."

Robert turned to Anne. "Perhaps you would come too? Being local, you'll know all the snags. Would you help me?"

"Of course," said Anne.

"Why don't we all go?" suggested Jack. "Make a real important expedition of it, with compasses and coolies. We could take a hamper of food and several bottles of wine and a tent, as well as a local guide . . ." Anne glanced at him in some surprise but it was Margot who broke the slightly uncomfortable silence.

"Oh, don't be so idiotic, Jack, your green eyes are showing. Now come and sit down, it's time we had something to eat."

She dominated the rest of the evening, telling them of the various shows and vicissitudes she had been through. Her ankle was much better and soon she would be dancing again.

"That is, if she doesn't spend the summer here," thought Anne, thinking of the picnics Margot had proposed for Rawlinson Ground. Was she going to live there too? Surely she and Robert hadn't come to an understanding already?

Robert and Anne drove back to Lowater

in their respective cars, and arrived back at the same time.

"It's a sweet old house," said Robert as they came through the door, "I shall be sorry to leave—you and your mother have been so very kind and welcoming."

"Not at all," said Anne formally and then, more naturally, she added, "I wish you didn't feel you have to leave."

"Do you? I think it's best though." He caught hold of her hand. "Good night, sweet Anne."

His hand was warm and dry and for a moment they stood like that, hand-in-hand, still, silent, staring at each other. As though magnetised, they drew closer. He put his arms around her.

They heard footsteps on the flagged floor of the kitchen, the dogs came bounding out, followed more slowly by Barbara.

Robert bent down and fondled one of the dogs. He was yards away from Anne.

"Hello," Barbara said. "I've just been watching the most ridiculous thing on TV, heaven knows why. I should have gone to bed ages ago. Have you had a nice evening?"

Anne had previously phoned her to say

she was eating out, and Barbara obviously thought she and Robert had been having dinner on their own.

"We were at Cragfall, Mother" explained Anne patiently. "Margot has been looking at places for Robert to rent."

"Robert, my dear," Barbara protested. "You know you can stay here as long as you like."

"But I can't," Robert said. "I mustn't impose on your kindness any longer. A person can wear out his welcome, you know, can't he, Anne? And not always be saved by the bell," he added.

"I shall be most offended!" cried Barbara before Anne could say anything, "Both of us will be offended!"

"Dear Mrs. T, you mustn't be," said Robert. "I can't go on using Lowater like an hotel."

"Why not?" asked Barbara. "We've loved having a man about the place, haven't we, Anne?"

"Of course," said Anne. "I'm going to leave you two to argue it out. I'm going to bed."

She felt faint and disorientated. Had her mother seen them spring apart like scalded cats? She didn't think so. Oh, Robert, Robert, do you know how I feel about you —saved by the bell, indeed!

14

WITHIN the week, Robert had made his arrangements to move out of Lowater. He had spent a whole day looking at various places, and perhaps out of contrariness, he *had* made an expedition out of it. He had instructed Margot to pack a picnic basket. He then invited Anne and Jack to accompany them on their tour. They went to five or six places ending, rather exhausted, at Rawlinson Ground. This was the one Margot preferred and which she was sure Robert would, too.

Anne knew the house well. The Collins family had lived there for several generations and had been large landowners in the district at one time. But the last owner, unmarried, had sold his farms off piecemeal, and much of the furniture and paintings in the house, in order to live. When he died, in his eighties, some years ago, the house had become run-down and neglected. The nephew who had inherited paid it periodic visits and had now apparently decided to do something about it before it fell down from damp and dry rot and woodworm.

"Maybe we'll be able to picnic by the lake," said Margot happily. "It's such a beautiful day." She waved at the blue, blue sky as though she had ordained the weather herself. It was another fine day in this spring of fine days, thought Anne, but then it was often very beautiful at this time of the year, promising a lovely summer which often didn't materialise.

The odd-job-man, carrying a spade, came from behind a corner of the house to greet them, although that was hardly an appropriate word since it intimates some sort of welcome, and there was nothing welcoming about his manner.

He nodded at Margot, evidently recognising her from her previous visit, nodded again at Robert and the others when she introduced them, and stumped back into the house, after signalling them wordlessly to follow him.

His face was reddish-brown and weather-beaten with craggy, even features. He must have been a goodlooking young man. He had a pair of very blue eyes, a thatch of silvery hair, and his clothes looked very old indeed, more like a baggy second skin moulded to his shape. His hands were large and work-worn, almost like implements in themselves, Anne thought, as he put down his spade and pulled out a big heavy key from an inner mysterious pocket, to unlock Robert's part of the house.

Margot had been right about the charm and atmosphere. Robert's main room was the old drawing-room, with a polished oak-strip floor and long windows which overlooked smooth lawns leading down to the water. The bedrooms and bathroom and kitchen were adequate enough if nothing to shriek about. The place was, as Margot described, very sparsely furnished but this somehow added to its charm rather than detracted from it. It had a waiting, an anticipatory air, attendant on someone to fill the silence.

Margot limped about, waving her arms and pointing out the advantages, watched intently and impassively by the odd-job-man.

"You can take these curtains down," she

said, indicating some very faded silk which hung at the windows. "Buy some beautiful chintz—I'll choose a lovely traditional pattern for you."

"It's all right as it is," Robert said easily. "I'm not sure I want to settle so permanently that I'll be buying chintz. What do you think of the place, Anne? Do you approve?"

Anne nodded her head. He would think she was daft if she said she thought it was full of ghosts—but it *was* charming and the views from the windows of the water with the trees in the distance were lovely.

She had seen hardly anything of him these past few days. He had spent very little time in the office; he was never at home at Lowater in the evenings. She would almost swear that he had been deliberately avoiding her. In case he had given her a wrong impression?

"Well, let's go and have our picnic, said Margot "I'm starving."

"The gardens are beautiful." Anne turned to the odd-job-man. "You must spend a lot of time on them, Mr—?"

He nodded. "Aye. Lewthwaite's my name."

"Will it be all right if we go and picnic down by the water, Mr. Lewthwaite?" Anne asked him politely.

He looked at her doubtfully and then glanced at the others. "Aye," he said at length, "but pick up your litter."

"Oh, we won't leave any."

"Put your car in the yard," he said more graciously. "I shouldn't leave it in the road," he added. "There's a terrible lot of traffic today—and a lot of folk about."

"Holiday makers?" suggested Anne.

"Nay," he said sombrely. "I don't give owt to them as folk. It's Mrs. Postlethwaite down the road. She's having a coffee morning in aid of the NSPCC."

They walked sedately down to the water, Jack and Robert bringing up the rear with the picnic basket and blankets to sit on.

"Did he mean he didn't class holiday-makers as folk?" asked Robert.

Anne laughed. "Yes, I suppose so— barely human. We should be flattered he doesn't think we're holidaymakers. Rather a dear old boy, isn't he? An old piece of Cumbrian rock!"

"How's he going to get on when the house is turned into holiday flats?" asked

Margot, "and he's got holiday-makers all over the place?"

"He'll enjoy himself giving a few pithy descriptions to his cronies, I'd guess," said Robert perceptively.

They found a smooth patch of greensward by the water's edge and in the sun, and spread their blankets. Margot presided over the unpacking of the picnic basket, doling out plates and knives and forks, arranging the food in the middle of the circle so that they could help themselves as they felt like it.

After they had eaten, they lay somnolently for a while basking in the sun.

Then Jack got up in a restless kind of way and walked to the edge of the water, watching a dinghy sailing past, looking, with its small white sail, like a toy in a bath.

"You could have a boat, Robert," said Margot, "A nice little cruiser."

"Motor boats on the lake aren't allowed," said Anne. "You'll have to go to Windermere if you want a cruiser."

"Spoilsport," said Margot.

"Spoiling it for whom?" asked Anne.

"It's so quiet and peaceful here, without a lot of engine noises."

"I don't want a motor boat," said Robert. "Maybe a punt or a row-boat."

"You could fish for char then," said Anne.

"Char? What's that?" asked Margot.

"A rather delicious little fish, pink-fleshed, which only lives in deep, cold water, and is native to these parts," Anne explained.

Margot rose to her feet and walked after Jack. Her limp was much less pronounced. Maybe Margot would be leaving soon, going away to dance. "I do not think I will miss her much," thought Anne, "although I suppose her enthusiasm and energy are refreshing."

Robert lay back and closed his eyes. "Would you come fishing for char with me, Anne?"

"You must get your boat first," she answered lightly, looking at him. There was more to his face than good looks. There was a strength there. He would be a support in times of trouble. Was he really falling for Margot? And yet James Millard thought he was interested in Natalie. She could well understand James wanting him for a son-in-law. He made you understand why people found charisma such a useful word. It covered so many attributes.

"A penny for them," he said suddenly, "Or should it be five pence, allowing for inflation?" He opened his eyes and sat up.

"I wasn't thinking of anything much," Anne lied, "—only how nice it is here— how beautiful the water and the sky and the trees—" she gave an all-enveloping sweep to her surroundings with her arms. "Are you going to take this place?"

"I expect so," he said.

He moved a few days later.

Seeing him off the premises, with Anne by her side, Barbara said, "I am sorry you're going."

"You haven't got rid of me for ever," he said and kissed her affectionately on her cheek. Anne moved away from her mother's side. "You can't get out of it like that," he said and he kissed her too, quite deliberately and hard on the mouth. "See you at the office later."

He turned and climbed into his car and swept off down the drive. Barbara glanced quickly at her daughter, sensing some frisson in the atmosphere, but Anne's expression was impassive and uncommunicative.

She didn't see much of Robert in the next few weeks. He was busy most days at Hunthorpe and only came in to see to his mail and dictate to Beryl. But he was seeing quite a lot of Margot, Anne knew.

"She's busy making Rawlinson Ground comfortable for Robert," Jack told her. "God knows what she does there. I suppose she's being the busy little domestic. I've told her it doesn't suit her."

As yet, Anne had not been able to bring herself to talk to Jack, to tell him her feelings really and truthfully had changed.

Every morning she awoke with the resolution that today she would talk to him, explain herself, ask him to understand and stay friends.

Every day she failed to bring herself to the point. It was cowardice, she knew. Then she had a reprieve.

Jack was going to London. He had business there, he explained to Anne. And he had to see his daughter, Karen. He wouldn't be away long.

"Will you bring Karen back with you?" asked Anne.

"I don't think so," Jack said evasively. "She'll be at school and her mother probably has other arrangements for the holidays. But I'll be back pretty soon."

"What about Margot?" asked Anne.

"Oh, she's staying on for a bit," Jack said. "Myra said she can stay on in the barn if she wants to, but it's my guess she'll be moving into Rawlinson Ground pretty soon. I've told her she spends so much time there, she might as well take her luggage with her!"

Her mother also went to London to stay with James for a week or so in his London flat. "We've got such a lot of things to discuss and plan," her mother said happily, "and there is also the final paperwork about the take-over of *Grandma Tyson*. It's easier for me to sign things in London, but I shall keep you posted on every detail, Anne, and tell you of the final arrangements. I want to discuss everything with Sarah and Jenny too. I think Sarah and Bobby might prefer me to settle money on the children instead of themselves but Jenny, like you, can have a lump sum."

In a very short while, the take-over became a fact. *Grandma Tyson* was now part of the great combine of Warings Foods. Barbara settled cash and shares on each of her daughters; Anne was given a new title. She was to be the Managing Director of *Grandma Tyson*, Robert Fordham was Chairman. Two outside directors were appointed to the board.

To begin with, there were only small signs of *Grandma Tyson's* changed status. There were suggestions for a refurbishment of the premises, some rebuilding at the back where space allowed. An architect employed by Warings came to look round, the time and motion study team arrived. It was this team which gave Anne the greatest misgiving. She might have a fancy new title but her own job had not changed much. She carried on exactly as she had before but the time and motion team seemed to presage a new era.

The team consisted of three people: an earnest, spectacled man called, suitably, Ernest Fanshaw, an earnest, spectacled girl called Lucy Taylor, and another more cheerful and casual man, Jimmy Landon. He talked at length to Anne and Beryl about his job, seeming to assume enormous changes would take place in the running and manning of the factory, and taking their acquiescence in these changes as a foregone conclusion. His two colleagues were more reticent and Anne discounted much of Jimmy Landon's remarks. He was a chatterbox and he exaggerated. The three of them took some time going round the factory, talking to the workforce individually.

Anne and Beryl watched them one day from the office window which overlooked the bakehouse. The team seemed to fill unnumerable clip-boards with their notes. At the end, apparently, they would go away, digest them, and make a report.

"And what then?" asked Beryl.

"We become more efficient," said Anne.

"I think we're perfectly all right as we are," said Beryl. "They're quite nice people, but they do seem to have been asking the most strange questions which don't seem very relevant to the uninitiated."

The pair of them were sitting companionably in Anne's office having a cup of tea and a gossip.

The door opened and Robert appeared, surprising them both. He had been all day at Hunthorpe and they were not expecting him back.

"Tea! Tea!" he said staring at their cups.

"Would you like some?" Beryl got up and hurried next door to find a clean mug. Robert had won Beryl over completely. She thought he was lovely and worked hard to please him.

Robert sat down in the chair the other side of Anne's desk and leaned back.

"I hear the lemon has abandoned you," he said.

Anne, ruffled, said, "If you are referring to Jack, your news is out of date. He's been gone ten days and I am expecting him back at any time."

"So he's not abandoned you? I was misinformed? Why wasn't I told he'd gone away? I'd have taken advantage of his absence."

And when she stayed silent, he said "Come and have supper with me tonight. Margot is cooking it. We've asked the time and motion lot over as it's their last night."

"I . . ." began Anne.

"That's settled then." Robert took the

mug of tea Beryl proffered at this juncture. "Shall I come over and pick you up? About seven-thirty?"

"I think I can manage to drive myself."

Anne was irritated by her ambivalent feelings towards the invitation. She wanted to go and see how he had settled into Rawlinson Ground, and she didn't want to go near the place. While Jack had been away, she had had no contact with Margot and her curiosity had been unassuaged and, despite her efforts at controlling it, had continued unabated.

The feeling of ambivalence persisted when she changed her clothes for the evening. She wanted to look her prettiest and she didn't want anyone to think she had made a supreme effort. Common sense asserted itself. Robert Fordham only had the power to get under skin like this if she let him. She wanted to look her best for her own satisfaction. "And not to compete with the glamorous Margot?"—a little inner scoffing voice interrupted.

Defying the scoffing voice, she pinned her hair up in a new style, wore a pretty skirt with a new frilly white blouse her mother had sent her from London. She looked quite different, she thought, gazing at her reflection in the mirror, much more sophisticated, and, yes, dashing.

Robert came outside to greet her when she arrived at Rawlinson Ground. Something flickered in his eyes when he saw her, but whether it was surprise at her different appearance or admiration at the change, she could not tell. He did not remark on it but led her inside.

Margot was not so reticent. "Hey, hey!" she said. "What's happened to our Miss Mouse? Where did you get that lovely blouse?"

She did not wait for an answer but walked across the room to the French windows leading into the garden.

It would be hard to compete with Margot, Anne conceded. Her ankle was now much better and she moved gracefully across the drawing-room, attired in a loose, floating sort of dress, patterned in a rainbow of colours, literally shading like a rainbow across her bosom and fading away into the skirt.

It was a beautiful, tranquil, late spring evening and the other guests, the time and motion team, were having their pre-dinner drinks on the terrace overlooking the water.

The lake was a mirror with sharp reflections from the trees on the shore and the little boats moored to the jetty.

"Isn't it beautiful?" asked Margot. "You know, Robert and I just sit for hours sometimes in the evening, just looking at the water, and the sky—they change colour so many times it is more beautiful than any painting."

She had made them an easy, pleasant meal, half-cold, half-hot, and she sat at the other end of the table from Robert, very much the hostess. Perhaps she had taken Jack's advice and moved into Rawlinson Ground. The thought gave Anne a pang, and took away her appetite. She must not, she did not care what Robert Fordham did or whom he lived with.

She was sitting on his left at the table and she turned away from him and began talking to the earnest Ernest.

"I hope you have enjoyed being here," she said politely.

"I suppose it's better than Saudi Arabia," he said. "We travel around a bit, you know." He made her feel she had been patronising.

"This is quite a small job for us really, considering," Ernest went on, finally putting her in her place. "It shouldn't take us long to get our report out, and then you'll be able to take it from there."

"And we'll become marvellously efficient?" asked Anne.

"Well, you're not quite in the twentieth century, you know," said Ernest, smiling. "I didn't know such an old-fashioned enterprise could be so profitable, but judging from the return on capital, it's not too bad. But I think we'll be able to offer a few useful suggestions which will upgrade the way for alterations and expansion."

"Over my dead body," Anne thought.

Robert had overheard Ernest's last remarks. He caught Anne's eye. "Battles ahead?"

"Why should there be?"

"Why indeed? I don't want to fight with you." He gave her one of his hard, direct looks and she was the first to look away and stare unseeingly instead at her wine-glass, twisting its stem with nervy fingers.

He spoke to her no more during the rest

of the evening, giving his attention solely to his other guests. After dinner it was too cool to sit outside, so they had their coffee in the drawing-room. There were evidences of Margot's presence here, Anne noted—two lamps which Margot said she had converted out of two old vases bought at the antique stall in the market, several flowering plants, and a great big arrangement of flowers on a low table.

The others rose early to go. They wanted to make an early start in the morning as they were driving back to London.

Anne rose and followed them. The evening had been stale and unprofitable and she wished she hadn't come. Robert met her in the darkness of the hall. He put a restraining hand on her shoulder. "Don't go yet," he said. They could hear Margot in the driveway saying goodbye.

"Please, I must go—I have to be up early too," Anne said. He drew her closer to him, she felt his hands move up her arms. He pulled her closer still, unresisting, towards him. She put her hands up against his chest to push him away. Instead she stayed like that for an aeon, an eternity, staring up at his face, shadowed in the half-darkness.

What did he want of her? The air seemed palpably thick with tension, with electricity. If sparks had come out of her head, she would not have been surprised.

"Where are you, Robert?" She could hear Margot calling, as if from far away. "Robert! They're leaving!"

Robert broke away from her and joined Margot outside on the drive.

Anne picked up the shawl she had brought and pulled it round herself and followed more slowly. Her heart was beating uncontrollably fast.

She managed to make her goodbyes to Margot, to thank her sedately for the lovely evening.

Robert followed her to her car and opened the door for her. He seemed perfectly calm and controlled. Had she imagined that extraordinary electrical tension between them? Was she going mad? Having the vapours like some sex-starved female of past centuries because the curate spoke to her?

Robert put a finger under her chin and lifted her face. "Good night, Anne. Sleep well," he said, and dropped a swift, soft kiss on her mouth.

She got in the car and let down the window. "Thanks for the dinner," she called at his departing back. She caught a glimpse of his hand as he waved. She switched on her headlights and was off down the drive, revving her engine unnecessarily.

Driving home to Lowater, she decided she did not like Robert Fordham—no, that was putting it too mildly. She hated him. She hated his demeanour, the way he turned her legs to jelly, the way he first ignored her, then turned his attention on her like a searchlight. He knew his power. Margot and Beryl fawned over him, now he expected her to. Margot and Beryl, what odd companions. Anne giggled a little to herself at the thought of them lumped together. Neither of them would like such a pairing. She knew she was being ridiculous. He had aggravated her from the beginning. Tomorrow, when she met him in the office, she would be very cold and calm as though indifference was her middle name.

But Robert was not in the office in the morning. He had left a message with Beryl that he would be coming in later. But before that, Jack turned up without warning. He gave her a big, boisterous kiss in front of Beryl.

"Have you missed me?" he asked.

"Of course," said Anne, ashamed of her lie. His absence had been a solace. Now she had to face up to her commitment to him.

"I've got something to show you," said Jack mysteriously. "Come into the yard."

Obediently Anne followed him downstairs.

Standing in the yard, in a dazzle of chrome glory, was an enormous motorised caravan. To Anne's astonished eyes, it looked the size of a coach.

"Mine!" said Jack proudly. "I was going to get a trailer caravan and then I thought this a much better idea so I sold my car . . ."

"But it's so huge—" said Anne at length.

"It's for our tour round the world," said Jack. "Come inside and see all the fixtures and fittings."

Bemused, Anne went up the steps and was shown the galley, the clever way the sofa folded out to make a double bed, the fridge, the shower . . .

"Isn't it difficult to drive?" she asked. It was like one of the gypsy caravans at Appleby Fair, she thought. All it needed was the set of Crown Derby and the crystal glasses arranged on the glass-fronted shelves of the store-cupboards.

"It takes a bit of getting used to," admitted Jack, "but I found it pretty easy on the motorway."

Robert drove into the yard at that moment. He parked his car and came over and joined them.

"It's for our wedding trip," Jack said. "For our Grand Tour. We'll be completely independent of hotels—just go where we like, when we like . . ."

"You'll need some good roads," Robert said.

"It's quite easy to drive once you get used to it," said Jack confidently. "Even Natalie had a go driving it."

"Natalie?" said Anne in amazement.

"I bumped into her at Danny's Disco—" Jack said quickly. "Wasn't it a coincidence? And I took her out a couple of times and she came with me to buy Ermentrude."

"Ermentrude?"

Jack laughed, "Well, Natalie christened

271

her that. We thought she ought to have a grand, dignified name. I suppose I had better get back to Cragfall. I drove straight here so that I could introduce you to Ermentrude."

Robert and Anne watched in silence while he manoeuvred the great shining vehicle out of the yard.

"I thought you promised to stay with me a year," Robert said grimly.

"I am staying a year."

"Jack talks as if you are going on your wedding trip next week."

Anne shrugged helplessly. "He knows I am going to stay a year."

She thought the caravan was a monster. The thought of driving round England or foreign parts in that great coach, glittering and shining like some fairground fantasy, gave her the shivers.

An old loyalty to Jack kept her from voicing any of these misgivings to Robert and she followed him silently back into the office.

She went to Cragfall straight after work. The beast, as she was to persist in calling Ermentrude to herself, was parked in the yard. It looked more incongruous still against this mossy, stony, rural background.

Myra was in the yard feeding the chickens. With her apron hitched over her ample skirts, her loose, flowing hair, the swill full of grain balanced on her hip, she looked like some earth mother, or possibly some goddess from the harvest festival.

Anne recognised the swill as one she had obtained for Myra. It was a local oval basket, coracle-shaped, made from split hazel and oak. At one time every village had its swill-maker, and swills were exported all over the north of England. Now the craft was dying out but a few old men, here and there, still made them. The baskets were very practical as well as attractive, with a multitude of uses. Myra, engrossed in handicrafts of all kinds as she was, had been anxious to acquire one. Anne knew a source and got her one. Now she was using it, as many farmers' wives before her had used it, to hold the grain as she fed the chickens.

Myra raised her eyes to heaven when she saw Anne. "Jack's off his rocker," she said. "Why ever did you let him buy that horrible thing?"

"I didn't have much say," said Anne.

"But where on earth did he get the money?" asked Myra "It must have cost thousands."

"He sold his car."

"That old heap wasn't worth anything," Myra said. "This must have cost as much as a Rolls Royce. If he wants to be a gypsy, why couldn't he get a nice little caravan on wheels to tow?—Or buy a real gypsy caravan, with a horse, and painted lovely colours . . ."

"The coach will be more comfortable," suggested Anne loyally but without conviction. She was never, however much she tried, going to be able to raise any enthusiasm for travelling in Ermentrude.

"I can't stand the sight of it," said Myra. "It takes up too much room in the yard. How long will it be parked here, do you think? When are you going on your trip?"

"Not for a while," said Anne weakly.

"Does he think he's going to leave it here for months?" demanded Myra. "I can't imagine why you spent your money on such a thing, Anne!"

"I didn't spend my money . . ." Anne began.

"Well, where did he get the money?"

Anne shrugged. "I don't know. He has money of his own."

"He hasn't a sou," said Myra. "Why do you suppose we let him have the barn all this time, paying no rent? It's so typical of Jack. You try to help, and he always overdoes it and takes advantage of your good nature." She threw a last handful of grain at the hens pecking round her feet and stomped back into the house. She was obviously rather put out.

Anne climbed up the stairs of the barn to see Jack.

15

JACK was sprawled back in one of the sag-bags watching the television news when Anne entered the barn.

"Hi, hello there," he said. "I wasn't expecting you so soon." He rose lazily to his feet and switched off the TV. Sudden silence descended.

"Would you like a drink?" he asked.

Anne shook her head. "Jack, I must talk to you." All the way there, she had been trying to plan, to think what she was going to say, but now the words seemed to have left her head.

"Well, I'm going to have one," he said, going over to the drinks table and splashing soda water and ice into a glass of whisky.

"Jack," said Anne gently, "don't you think you've been a bit premature in buying Ermentrude? We won't be going away for months."

"I expect to leave in one or two," he said with emphasis, "immediately after we're married."

"But, Jack, I told you I'd promised my mother I'd go on working for a year," Anne said.

"Bully for her," said Jack. "She decides to get married, you stay behind to mind the store like a skivvy. I think it's time you told your mother where she gets off," and when Anne was silent, he went on, "Don't you see, Anne, you let everyone tread all over you? You're such a doormat. I offer you an exciting prospect to see the world, and you examine the idea like an old woman. Haven't you got any imagination? Don't you want life to be exciting?"

"I find life exciting enough," she said faintly. "Where did you get the money to buy Ermentrude?"

"I put up some and I borrowed the rest," said Jack, after a pause. "I'm hoping that you will be paying off my loan."

"And what do we use for money on this trip?" asked Anne.

"Well, you've got plenty, haven't you?"

"I haven't a bottomless purse . . . what do we do when it's all spent . . .?"

"Money should be the least of our worries," Jack cried. "Life is so boring,

Anne, sitting in this dull spot, month after month."

"It isn't a dull spot," Anne protested. "It's a beautiful place."

"Oh, you can keep the nature bit. Don't go and sound off like Myra."

"I don't see what's exciting about sitting in that ghastly coach, staring at foreign people and foreign scenes, always the onlooker, the spectator . . . dreadful. I don't want to watch all the time . . . I like to do things, to make things . . ."

"Such as biscuits?" he flung at her contemptuously.

"You don't mind taking advantage of such an enterprise, using the money which came from biscuits. I think it's a monstrous suggestion to use my mother's money in such a way."

"What do you want to do with it? Give it to the starving millions in Africa? Or is it because I propose to live on your money that you're so offended? If I were a rich man, and you were poor, and we got married, would you not live on my money? With no qualms? Why should I keep you if you are not prepared to keep me? What is sauce for the goose is also sauce for the gander, my dear girl! Or aren't you as liberated as all that? I don't believe in your puritanical work ethic that work's good for work's sake . . ." he flung himself about the barn, like a frenzied small boy, finally sitting down again, his face set in cross, sulky lines.

Once that little-boy-lost quality had been part of his charm, Anne thought. Like a mother, she had wanted to put things right for him. He had traded on that maternal instinct: now she was being asked to provide more for him—his idea of an exciting life, continual motion. It was not hers.

She said slowly, "If I got married, I do not think I would like always to be dependent on my husband. I think I would always value my independence, be my own woman as it were. I do not understand how you can sit there and propose so calmly to live off me. You emasculate yourself."

"Rubbish," said Jack. "I don't feel in the least emasculated." He jumped up and came and knelt at her feet. "Anne darling, I don't want to quarrel." He put his arms round her waist and tried to hug her to him. She resisted gently, taking his hands away. Once he had such power to stir her. Now she felt nothing but sadness. Her infatuation was over. She gave a small sigh for lost illusions and past happiness. Now she saw Jack clearly for what he was, a rather charming, vain and shallow man, both irrational and rash. There would be other women to console and forgive him, stronger than she was.

"I don't want to quarrel with you either," she said, "but it's no good, Jack. We are never going to see eye to eye over important things. Or even trivial ones." She slipped her pretty engagement ring off her finger. "I think you had better have this back."

"Okay." He put it nonchalantly into the pocket of his jeans. "I daresay I'll find a use for it. You're not the only string to my bow, Anne dear. I've got an ace in the hole. Your prissiness has been rather a pain for some time. Go and stuff your head in your biscuit mix for all I care."

Wounded, Anne rose stiffly to her feet. "Goodbye, Jack." He said nothing, just stared at her, his expression sneering.

Driving home to Lowater, tears came into her eyes. She brushed them away with her hand impatiently. She was not going to cry over Jack. She had been incredibly naïve and foolish. "Methinks I was enamoured of an ass," she misquoted Titania to herself. Her mother would be pleased, she thought wryly. Overlying her sadness was a powerful feeling of relief. She had done it. She had broken off her engagement at last. She and Jack had never been right for each other. It was a fact she had shirked facing for too long. Because she did not want to admit she had been wrong and her mother had been right? Because she had been annoyed that Robert Fordham had said the same thing to her? She pushed the thought of Robert Fordham away from her. He was not likely to act as a tranquilliser to her feelings of disillusion and disappointment.

She drove up the lane to Lowater and put her car in the garage. Coming up to the house she was surprised to see her mother's car parked in front. A surprise visit? She had not said she was coming up.

Anne entered the house and called out, "Ma!" Nobody answered. She looked in the kitchen and the sitting-room but there was no one there. She went up the stairs. "Ma!"

As she came on to the landing, her mother came out of her bedroom. She came forward in a little rush and hugged Anne to her. "Oh, Anne, Anne!"

"Mother darling, what's the matter?" Anne held Barbara away from her. Her mother's eyes were red from weeping.

"When did you arrive? What has happened?"

"I've had a row with James," her mother said. "I just had to get away. I couldn't stand it a minute longer. I drove up this afternoon. James didn't know I was coming. I left a note for him."

"Oh, Mother darling, come and tell me about it," Anne said softly, as though her mother was her child. "Can I get you a drink? Would you like a cup of tea?"

"I don't want anything. I made myself some tea, or at least Maureen made me some. She was here when I arrived. I am afraid I broke down when she left . . . so stupid . . . but I feel such a fool . . . How are you, Anne dear? You look very well—"

"I'm fine," Anne said. Her mother was

clearly too distressed to hear any more woes.

Later, over a drink, her mother was calmer.

"Everything was lovely at first," she said. "I stayed in the flat with James. I love him very much and I think his affection for me is genuine. At the weekend we went to Grayham and that was lovely too. We had a most idyllic time. Natalie was there, of course and, in the beginning, she was very sweet and charming, and then gradually she began to change. You see, she has been the apple of her father's eye. They have spent a lot of time together and she began to be jealous. I understand—at least I understood—her jealousy. It was perfectly natural. I tried to show her there was no real reason for it.

"At first I don't think she realised how her father's life was going to be changed by my presence. After all, Natalie has acted as his hostess many times—for business as well as social entertaining—and, of course, she is pretty and charming . . . and she has been made much of. Now her nose was slightly out of joint, and I am afraid she didn't like it. Incidentally, she saw quite a lot of Jack Cooper when he was in London."

"Yes, I know," said Anne, composedly.

"Can you imagine? I was quite delighted to see Jack! She was so much nicer when he was around. I actually encouraged him to come to the flat. I really don't think she has enough friends of her own age—or else in the past, she hasn't wanted them. Anyway, things got worse and worse between us. She told me that James had only bought *Grandma Tyson* because he felt sorry for me working so hard, that he had no interest in the place . . ."

"How ridiculous," protested Anne. "He's not that quixotic!"

"No," agreed her mother a little doubtfully. "Anyway, I at last began to see that I was going to be the dreaded bogey stepmother. We've never had that kind of family life, with awful atmospheres—and people slamming out of the room in a temper . . ."

"Oh, no?" asked Anne with a smile. "I seem to remember arguments among us all."

"Not like this," her mother said. "There was never any hate."

"And what about James in all this?"

"He didn't seem to mind as much as I did. I don't, anyway, think he knew half of what was going on. Natalie used to keep her sharpest utterances for when he wasn't there. And I wasn't going to tell tales. Besides, he says Natalie has always been temperamental . . ."

"Spoilt, he means," said Anne drily. "Natalie is young, she'll be getting married one of these days . . . with a life of her own . . . she might become more understanding . . ."

"Perhaps," said Barbara slowly. "I do love James and we could have a wonderful life together, but I am not going to have it spoilt for both of us by Natalie."

"But what happened?"

"Natalie and I had a real rip-roaring showdown—it had been building up for days—and I told her a few home truths she didn't in the least like hearing . . . James joined in . . . I think we all said a lot we didn't mean . . . and so I decided to clear off and have a breathing space and a breath of lovely fresh air . . . London can be a bit stifling. Have I been silly?"

Anne hugged her mother to her.

"Probably," she said, "But I expect you cleared the air. You never were one for bottling things up!"

They talked a little about *Grandma Tyson*, and Anne told her mother about the time and motion team, and various new business which had come their way. She gave her the gossip about life around— Maureen's sister was emigrating to Canada —her husband had been offered a very good job—and her Grandad was in hospital —she'd sent him some books and fruit— and Mrs. Redhead was having a baby— and they'd done very well with the wethers they'd sent to market. But she kept the news about Jack to herself. Her mother would be pleased, she knew, and it was mean not to tell her, but for the moment she did not feel she could cope with her mother's reception of the news which would be exuberant.

"Will you come to the factory tomorrow to see Beryl and have a look round?" Anne asked.

"I don't think so," her mother said. "I thought I'd drive up to Carlisle. Dorrie Dixon wrote to me and told me about her show of paintings so I thought I'd go to that and then see Dorrie afterwards." Dorrie was an old friend of twenty years' standing, a talented painter of portraits and a very down-to-earth, comforting sort of person. Yes, thought Anne, that was a good idea. "I might stay the night," her mother went on, "and come back the next morning. I'll pay a grand visit to the factory next week."

The next morning, she looked very much more composed and very smart, dressed in the new clothes she had bought in London. She gave Anne a cheerful wave as she drove off but Anne was still a little worrried about her as she went to work.

Driving along, Anne also worried about Jack. She had hated parting from him in that cold, civilised way last night. Had he got into terrible debt over the beastly Ermentrude? Ought she anyway to offer to pay something towards it? She could, she supposed, and surely he would be able to sell it. She owed him that perhaps. How foolish can you get? But foolish or not, to salve her conscience, Anne turned up the lane which led to Cragfall.

There was no one in the yard, and no sign of Ermentrude. Perhaps he had parked the beast out of sight behind the barn. Anne looked, but the coach was nowhere to be seen. She went up the steps into the barn, but the place was empty.

Anne went downstairs again and across the yard, and knocked at the Brackens' old oak door. One of the Bracken toddlers opened it and stared at her with wondering eyes. She ran off and called her mother and a few seconds later Myra came out of the kitchen. "Keep an eye on the toast," she called over her shoulder. From the pleasant smell of bacon in the air, Anne guessed Myra was cooking breakfast.

"I came to see Jack," Anne said.

"Jack? But he went last night," Myra answered.

"Went where?"

"He went back to London."

"In that coach thing?"

"Yes, thank God. He left soon after you did last night. I thought you were going with him?"

"No."

Myra stared at her. "I'm terribly sorry —if it's a surprise, or a shock."

"It's a surprise," said Anne. "I didn't think he would leave so soon."

288

"I'm sorry," said Myra.

"You don't have to be sorry for me," said Anne quickly, "I broke off our engagement last night."

"Oh dear," Myra said. "Has he gone off in a huff, do you think?"

"Who knows?" said Anne. "I don't think he cared very much."

"We worried about you," Myra said, "Jack's had a lot of girlfriends, but you seemed so stable, as well as attractive, and George said everyone has to settle down sometime, and maybe Jack was ready to. His wife left him, you know. She couldn't stand the uncertainty of life with him, not knowing where he was or with whom, or whether she would get any housekeeping. She got fed up in the end and left him and took a job. They're still friends. Margot was an ex-girlfriend—very ex—but I suppose you knew that."

"Where is Margot?" asked Anne. "Did she go with him?"

"She left a couple of days ago," said Myra. "She went off to stay at Rawlinson Ground. I think it was just a little more comfortable than the barn!" She laughed. "And, of course, there was the attraction of Robert Fordham. He's quite a dish, isn't he?"

"Yes," said Anne mechanically, "Quite a dish. I must go now."

"You're not upset?" Myra asked, looking more closely at her. "You're rather pale. Have some breakfast with us."

"No thank you. I'm not upset. I was just worried a bit about Jack, buying that horrible Ermentrude and borrowing money to do it . . . I thought maybe it was my fault, my responsibility . . ."

"Don't worry about Jack," said Myra heartily. "None of his friends worries about Jack. He's well able to look after himself. He always falls on his feet—oh, my lord, the toast! Can you smell it?" She rushed back into the kitchen.

Anne called out "Goodbye" to her disappearing back, and climbed into her car and drove off to work.

She drove on, her head a turmoil of thoughts. Regrets about Jack and her own stupidity mingled with thoughts of Robert and Margot. So she had been right the other night when she thought Margot had moved into Rawlinson Ground.

As she drove into the factory yard, she

noticed several little knots of women workers, attired in their familiar blue-checked overalls and caps, hanging about. One lot, when they saw her, tumbled themselves hurriedly back inside. Surely she wasn't as late as all that? It wasn't time for their break yet. What were they doing outside at this hour?

She went into the bakehouse. Here there was not the usual hum of activity. More knots of men stood idle by the ovens. There were no girls packing the biscuits, no men at the other end feeding the chutes and the mixing machines. Whatever was the matter? She looked around in surprise and many of the men and women turned away from her as though unable to meet her eyes.

She turned to the grizzled old foreman who was standing near the main oven in the middle of the room.

"Tom," she said. "What's the matter? Why isn't anybody working?"

He stared down at his feet for a moment, then raised his head and gave her a brave look from his blue eyes. "They're on strike, Miss Anne," he said almost apologetically.

"On strike?" For a moment, Anne was

silent with surprise. "But what for?" she asked when she had got her breath back.

"There's some talk going around that there are going to be a lot of sackings now we're Warings," he said, "and different ways of working, faster like, more automated like . . ."

"That's rubbish," Anne said. "There have been no suggestions of any changes as yet. I would be the first to know about them. We are going on exactly as we have been for the past twenty years."

"Well, there's the new place at Hunthorpe," Tom went on, "and they're using a lot of new machinery there which doesn't need so many hands . . ."

"Whatever is going on at Hunthorpe is nothing to do with us," Anne said. She gave a swift glance round the room. "Is everyone on strike?" she asked.

"Well, some haven't turned up," Tom said. "There was a bit of talk about it yesterday. The ones who have come are the most militant, I think, they wanted to make a point."

"And you? Tom, are you on strike, after all these years?"

He was silent. "I find that very hurtful,"

she said, "You could have come and asked what was going on. I find all this very hurtful."

She turned away and went upstairs to her office. Beryl was not there. She could hear the murmur of Robert's voice, dictating, so presumably she was with him. She looked in the little office shared by the two girls who helped Beryl. They stopped typing when they saw her, and looked solemnly at her like sheep in a field, interrupted in their grazing. Anne stared solemnly back at them. At least they weren't on strike. She shut the door without a word and she heard the clacking of their typewriters re-start.

Nonplussed, Anne sat down at her desk. What was she to do? What insane idea had possessed those fools in the bakehouse? Who had been spreading rumours? Or had they just floated out of the air because of Hunthorpe, because of that stupid time and motion team and their silly questions, and people putting two and two together and making five, and passing it on and making seven . . ?

The door of her office opened suddenly and Robert stood there. "Where the hell have you been?" he asked angrily, "We've been ringing all over for you."

Staring at his unsympathetic, grim face, everything suddenly seemed too much for Anne.

She gave a strangled sob, put her arms on her desk, buried her face in them and burst into tears.

"That's all we need," Robert said. "Anne, for heaven's sake, pull yourself together. I'm sorry I shouted at you . . . It's not the end of the world . . ."

"Oh, shut up," Anne cried in a muffled voice, hiccoughing with sobs. "It's nothing to do with you . . . it's Jack . . . my mother . . . the strike . . ." she wailed incoherently.

He pulled her arms away from her face and dragged her to her feet. "Anne darling, I didn't mean to bark at you. I know this strike isn't your fault . . ."

"Of course, it's not," she said struggling to free herself, "Where's my handbag? I want a handkerchief."

He pulled a clean, folded handkerchief out of his pocket and put it up to her face and wiped it. "Come now, blow your nose, and tell me what this is all about." He looked across the desk, "Beryl love, go and get us all some tea."

Anne took the handkerchief from him, wiped her face again and blew her nose and sat down at her desk.

"What's going on?" asked Robert.

"How do I know? They were all right yesterday. I was not aware of any mutterings or plans for a strike. I suppose you think I should have been."

"I don't think anything of the sort. Do you know what I think we should do now?" Robert said, and when she did not answer, he said, "I think we should shut the office and go on strike ourselves. Leave them to worry it out and play hookey for the day. What do you say, Beryl?" He looked up as Beryl came in with the steaming tea.

"I can't do that," said Anne. "I'm going down to talk to them."

"When you've had your tea," said Robert.

"All right, when I've had my tea, and fixed my face," Anne said. "I must look a fright."

"You look very pretty," said Robert unexpectedly. "A bit pink about the eyes

295

perhaps. I've never seen anyone cry quite so prettily, have you, Beryl?"

"No," said Beryl, "But not everyone has Anne's advantage of a pretty face to begin with."

Anne took no notice of their gentle teasing but put her hand up to her head and hid her face behind it. She felt as if she was going to burst into tears again. But this, on top of everything else which had happened in the last two days, was more than she could bear.

"I mean what I said about the day off," said Robert softly. "It will do us both good. And how about you, Beryl? Couldn't you do with a day off?"

"There's a nice sale I wouldn't mind going to," said Beryl. "At least, it's the viewing day and I could leave a bid or two if I saw anything I fancied." One of Beryl's great loves was going to auction sales, and Anne smiled faintly.

"There, that's better," said Beryl. Anne got up and went to the cloakroom, washed her face, and re-did her make-up, and tried to make herself more presentable. She then went down to the bakehouse floor. Robert and Beryl watched her from the window in the office which overlooked it.

They saw her take a stand in the middle of the room, close by the biggest oven. She waved her arms, indicating that everyone was to draw closer to her. After an appreciable pause, her watchers saw the workers collect around her in a group. She was obviously talking to them but they could not hear what she was saying.

Anne stared round at *Grandma Tyson's* band of workers. Some of them belonged to a union, she knew, but they were not organised, but then there was nothing for them to organise themselves about. Their pay was somewhat higher than the average. From the beginning, her mother had always made that a rule. She wanted to attract the best; she wanted people to think working for *Grandma Tyson* was something special; she also wanted her workers to feel satisfied. There were regular bonuses when profits were good. Apart from this, their conditions of work were pleasant; there was a comfortable restroom, paid holidays and a contributory pension scheme. So in the past there had never been any trouble or unrest on the factory floor. Barbara was sure people were proud to work for *Grandma Tyson*.

She had told herself they were all one big happy family, and while perhaps not all the members of the "family" would have agreed with her, she and Anne knew the background of their workers in detail, remembering the births of children and grandchildren, who was related to whom— not always easy in the tangle of cousins and second-cousins. All these people she knew so well seemed to have turned themselves into an amorphous, hostile mob.

Anne fixed her eyes on Mrs. Hodgson, the same Mrs. Hodgson who all those weeks ago had wanted to be made redundant, and who had been persuaded against it, and who had given in agreeably when she heard that *Grandma Tyson* was to become part of Warings. Maybe she had thought her redundancy money would be greater; maybe she hadn't wanted to miss any of the spice the change might bring. Anne had always subscribed to the latter view. Mrs. Hodgson always liked to be in the thick of things, to know everything that was going on.

"I wish someone would tell me what this

is all about," said Anne, still looking at Mrs. Hodgson.

Mrs. Hodgson stared stolidly back. On this occasion, she was not going to utter.

Anne turned her gaze to another, younger woman, Olive Jackson who was, she knew, engaged to Stephen Sykes, one of the bakers in charge of the ovens.

"What is it all about?" Anne asked again. "Are you trying to be fashionable or something?"

There was a little titter. Olive Jackson went a little pinker, difficult since she had round rosy cheeks. Her skin was as fair as Anne's own.

"We don't like the changes," Olive said.

"But what changes?" asked Anne. "There haven't been any changes."

"Those chaps who came round," said Olive. "They said there were going to be all sorts of changes. That we wouldn't know what had hit us, that we'd have to come out of the Ark."

"They had no business to say that," said Anne crossly. "They are going to make suggestions as to how we can improve production—but that doesn't mean to say we are going to agree with them."

"Why come round then?"

"Why ask us all those questions?"

"'Antediluvian', the spectacled one said . . ."

"There's going to be a lot of rebuilding, the fat one said so . . ."

"We have to increase productivity— 'What's that,' I said . . ."

"London head office will be running things from now on . . ."

Everyone was talking at once in a great babble.

Anne raised her hand for silence. "There might be changes, there might not," she said, "but we're not going to be turned into some slick automated operation . . . Our whole purpose would be lost then. We are a small family business—we turn out a very good product which is not mass-produced —we're not competing with all the big firms under the Waring umbrella . . . All we get from being under that umbrella are advantages . . ."

"And what do Warings get from us?" asked someone.

"Aye, what do Warings get from us?" repeated someone else.

"A very good quality product," Anne

300

said quickly, "to add to the rest of their good products, and one which they are proud to put out," she paused, "And they get a very good return on their capital investment, which is what their shareholders are interested in." She took a deep breath. "I am in charge of *Grandma Tyson* now, and I know of no changes which are going to take place—and I will be the instigator of changes, so I should know. But I am going to make a suggestion— Why don't you choose someone amongst yourselves, or elect a representative—to sit on the board—then he or she can give their views, and yours, on any suggested changes which are put forward—and on our expansion? How about that?"

Heaven knows what the rest of the board will think of that, she said to herself, but she would cross that hurdle when she came to it.

"Please think it over. It's Friday today. We've lost a day's production anyway so I suggest you all take the rest of the day off —with pay," she added quickly, "—and come back fresh, and ready to work, on Monday." She turned on her heel and walked quickly away across the bakehouse floor up the stairs to her office.

Robert and Beryl turned away from the window as she came in and flopped into a chair.

"What did you say to them?" asked Beryl.

"I told them to take the day off." Anne glanced at Robert. "And I told them to elect a representative to sit on the board and discuss the changes with us. Am I mad? That is what they were worked up about. Your precious time and motion team put their backs up—but then southern city slickers always do, with us northern country bumpkins."

Robert was still standing by the window overlooking the bakehouse. "There seems to be a mighty lot of discussion going on . . . now the men are moving back to the chutes . . . they are going back to the mixing machines and the ovens . . ."

Anne got up and joined him by the window.

"They are going back to work!" she said. "They're not taking the day off, after all." As she watched, the men and girls took their accustomed places, turning themselves into people again. The hostile, amorphous mob had dissolved into individuals, with individual sorrows, hopes and happinesses.

Robert looked down at her. "Victory for you," he said gently, "But I still think you should take the day off, don't you, Beryl? She looks quite pale with exhaustion."

"Yes," said Beryl decisively. "Take the day off. I shall stay to keep an eye on things —blow that old auction, there's always another one."

There was a knock at the door. "Come in," Anne called. Tom, the foreman in charge of the ovens, stood outside.

He looked first at Robert and then at Anne. "Just came to tell you, Miss Anne, we thought we'd carry on. We'll be a bit behind but we think we might make it up with a bit of overtime." He did not wait for an answer but gave a kind of salute which comprehended all of them, and went downstairs.

"Total victory!" said Robert. "Come on, Anne, you deserve a day off." He turned to Beryl. "I think I dealt with all the mail that's urgent," he said. "If anyone phones, tell them—" he hesitated a moment and then added, "tell them I'm at a meeting with my Managing Director."

He followed Anne down the stairs. She stopped to face him in the yard. "But what are we going to do?" she asked helplessly. "We shouldn't be swanning off like this."

"I've bought a boat," said Robert looking down at her. "I thought we might go on the lake, take her on her maiden voyage. What I suggest is that you drive home, change into something more comfortable—you look too smart to go messing about in boats. I'll follow you and then we can drive to Rawlinson Ground together."

Anne drove back to Lowater in a kind of confused dream. She did not know why she had agreed to this truancy. She should be at *Grandma Tyson*. Whatever would her mother say when she heard that her beloved family had dared to strike? Ah, her mother. It would be a blow. And then there was Jack. She could not think of Jack now. Somehow she would have to get news to him that she would help him pay for the beastly Ermentrude and then her conscience would stay quiet.

She turned in at the gate of Lowater. In

her mirror she could see Robert's car close behind. He was being very kind but she did not need kindness. It would only make her burst into tears again.

She ran inside the house and upstairs. She changed quickly into jeans and a shirt, picked up a jersey in case it was cool on the water. It was a beautiful sunny day, the first true day of summer. There had been hints and promises before, but today the sun was bright and strong; there were pinks and peonies blooming in the garden and the striped, pale mauve clematis, dear Nelly Moser, was in flower among the yellow roses round the porch.

There were roses in bloom at Rawlinson Ground, too, and Mr. Lewthwaite was busy hoeing among them when they arrived. He gave them a friendly "good-morning," his blue eyes twinkling at Anne. "It's a grand day," he said.

Anne looked beyond him at the water, sparkling in the sunshine. "It's a grand day," she agreed.

"I'm going to change my clothes, too," said Robert. "Would you like some coffee or anything while you wait?"

"I don't think so." She followed him into

the house. Great shafts of sunshine splintered into the drawing-room.

"I won't be a second," Robert said and left her.

She wandered round the room, choosing to look at the few dark oil-paintings which decorated the walls. They all needed cleaning.

Robert came back. He carried a bottle of champagne in his hand. "I thought we ought to launch her properly," he said, "The boat, I mean."

"Oh, it's such a waste!" said Anne.

"I mean drink it, silly, not bash it over the bows," he said. "Anyway, the *Lotus Blossom* isn't new, although she's had such a great refurbish, she looks new."

"Where's Margot?" asked Anne. "Isn't she coming?"

"Margot?" Robert looked at her, puzzled. After a moment, he said, "She's gone. Didn't you know?"

"But when?"

"She left with your friends."

"My friends?"

"The city slickers, the time and motion team. Surely you heard her talking about it? She had a new job offered her and she left with them the morning after our dinner the other night. She talked about the new job all through dinner. Surely you heard her?"

"But I switched off that evening," thought Anne. Margot always did talk a lot about her dancing. Had she mentioned a new job? She could not remember.

"No doubt we will have the pleasure of seeing her dance on TV again one of these days—as a Gold Leopard or Black Panther or whatever," Robert said.

"I thought she was staying here," Anne said. "I thought you and Margot—" she stopped.

"Yes?" He suddenly sounded grim. "Staying here? She spent her last night at the pub with Landon and the others—so they could all make a very early start in the morning with no delay in picking her up from Cragfall. She never stayed here. I'm not exactly mad, you know, Anne. I don't generally lie down under steam-rollers."

Anne laughed. "So it's just us?"

"Just us."

A wave of pure unadulterated happiness had taken possession of her.

"I thought Margot would be coming to

help launch the boat. She's been very helpful."

"She's been very helpful," said Robert. "But she's had nothing to do with the boat."

While they had been talking, they had moved across the grass to the water. There, moored to the small wooden jetty, was a long, thin, rather rakish flat-bottomed boat, with a highly-varnished inside, and bright blue cushions at either end.

"It's a punt!" said Anne in mingled surprise and pleasure, "I thought at least it was going to be an enormous sailing boat like we had once, called *Herring Gull*, and my sisters and I could never manage it and were always arguing." She looked down at herself. "But I'm not properly dressed for it," she said, "I should be wearing a big hat and have a parasol . . ."

Robert laughed, "You look perfect to me. I'll have to row or paddle. The water's too deep for a pole. Do you like her? I think she's quite old, but the chap I got her from restored her and repainted her . . . and I renamed her, *Lotus Blossom*."

He held out his hand to her and she stepped carefully into the *Lotus Blossom*.

He handed her the champagne bottle and the two glasses he had also brought, and then stepped in himself. They sat down facing each other and Anne leaned against the cushions.

Robert unhooked the mooring chain, took hold of the oars and pushed away from the shore.

It was the beginning of a beautiful day.

Robert rowed with slow easy strokes towards the middle of the lake. There were no other boats about, no sailing dinghies, no people visible on the shore. It was as though they had the whole watery world to themselves. Beyond the long, smooth, glassy stretch of water, the mountains were hazy in the distance.

On the far shores on either side of them, the trees and greensward were the rich, bright, new green of early summer. Above them the sky was deep blue with not a cloud in sight.

Anne trailed her hand in the water. It was icy cold. After a while, Robert shipped his oars and they rocked gently in the middle of the lake.

"Do you want to tell me what's bothering

you?" he asked, "To ease your troubles by talking?"

Anne shook her head. "I just want to be," she said, "and not think about anything except this lovely day. Except perhaps one thing which I must tell you— mother has had a row with James. She came home last night."

"But why? I thought they were so happy."

"Natalie. She made things very uncomfortable."

After a silence in which Anne was remembering that he and Natalie had once been paired together so happily by Natalie's father, Robert said only, "Poor James!"

"And poor Mother too!"

Robert began rowing again. They were now gliding past the little island where Anne had landed so often when she was a child and played with her sisters.

"Would you like to see where we camped and played at castaways on a desert island?" she asked.

Robert headed the *Lotus Blossom* towards the island and beached her on the shingle. They scrambled ashore and Anne took him into the woody depths of the place and showed him the flat stones where they had made their fires, and cooked sausages and baked potatoes. The ground was black with recent use, so someone else still played the same games.

"It all seems much smaller," said Anne, when they had made the tour and seen the cave of rocks, and where they had made their tree-house. "It seemed like the jungle fifteen years ago."

They sat down on the rocks and Robert brought out the champagne which he had left cooling in the water, and the cork popped and they filled their glasses and toasted the *Lotus Blossom*.

"Did you go camping?" asked Anne, looking at him across her glass. "Where did you go for holidays as a child?" She accepted now that she was intensely curious about him, had always been, in a ridiculous manner. Everything about him was interesting—his size in socks—did he like garlic?—What did he read?—What music would he play on his desert island?

"Abroad mainly," Robert said. "We used to go to Italy—or France. My parents still do, although, of course, now they don't lie on a beach but go and look at libraries and art galleries."

"Where do they live?"

"In London. We're a very urban family. That's why I suppose all this—" he waved his hand at the scenery around him "has such an impact. It is such a different world, and a much pleasanter one. It's like being born again but with all your faculties—I see more here . . . I am more aware of living . . ."

"You don't think it's boring?"

"Boring? What a funny word to choose. No, nothing up here has been boring—as I think you must know, Anne." She met his glance. His eyes seemed to be burning with some intense emotion. He turned and picked up the champagne bottle. "Let's finish this off." He raised his glass, "To you, Anne, and your happiness."

She smiled to hide the sudden beating of her heart. At his kind tone, she felt the unwelcome tears flood into her eyes again. She tried to blink them back but they were like taps which refused to be turned off.

"I'm sorry to be so hysterical."

"Anne darling." He moved towards her and took her in his arms and cuddled her.

"Darling Anne, don't cry. Tell me what's bothering you . . . Are you worried about your mother?"

"No—I mean, yes—it's not that . . . I'm just being foolish . . ." she murmured incoherently.

He kissed her gently on her wet eyes, on her brow, her cheek and then on her mouth. At first his kisses were soft, butterfly touches but they became increasingly hard and urgent as his lips found hers, and some powerful force not to be gainsaid took possession of him. He crushed her to him and, entwined, they rolled over together on the grass. She heard the glasses tinkle and the champagne bottle crack as it rolled down the slope. She felt herself cling to him hungrily, faint and lost with the pleasure his kisses gave her.

At length he drew away from her. "I shouldn't have done that," he said huskily, sitting up and holding his head in his hands.

"I don't know what you should and shouldn't do," said Anne breathlessly. "You stopped me crying at all events."

He gave a short laugh, stood up and

pulled her to her feet. "We won't spoil this beautiful day," he said.

"But you're not spoiling it for me," Anne thought. She wanted his kisses. She wanted him to make love to her. Was that what she had wanted all along? Now she could admit it to herself. She wanted him to love her. She wanted to love him. She was in love with him. She had been, she guessed, for months without acknowledging it. Was she some feeble, emotional creature jumping from one love to the next in the wink of an eye? But no, she must not denigrate this and compare it with a lesser feeling. She had never felt this way about anyone before. The emotion she had once felt for Jack was a pale wraith beside this burning yearning which had taken hold of her.

"We must pick up our litter," said Robert as he collected champagne bottle and glasses, "or we'll have someone after us with a big stick."

They spent nearly the whole day on the water. At lunchtime they called at an old farmhouse which had a landing-stage. Anne had known the place when it was a farm; now the land was being farmed by a neighbour, and the house was a guest house with all the barns and outbuildings turned into accommodation. In the season, the proprietor served simple meals to non-residents. Anne was not sure the place was open yet but she thought they might be able to get some sandwiches. They were lucky and they took the sandwiches and some cans of beer back to the boat and sat there, companionably eating and drinking.

"Why does food always taste so ambrosial in the open air?" asked Robert. "These are just ordinary beef sandwiches —yet they taste extremely special."

"They are extremely special," said Anne, and added to herself, "—but that's because I'm eating them with you." Did he ever think about her? She knew now he was attracted to her—Or did he think of her as just another helpful creature, like Margot?

She wanted to tell him she had broken with Jack. She could not bring the words out. It would be tantamount to saying "*I am available now. I am not engaged.*" An invitation which he might not care to accept. What was a kiss, after all, between friends? Did it signify much or little?

They rowed back to Rawlinson Ground in the late afternoon, tired with the fresh air and a little sunburnt. It had been a beautiful day. Anne did not want it to end. Neither, it seemed, did Robert.

"Why don't we have a wash-and-brush-up," he suggested, "and then go somewhere for dinner? Can you make some suggestions? What about that nice place where you once took me to lunch?"

"Could I see first what my mother is doing?" asked Anne.

While he went and changed his clothes, she rang home, and was told by Maureen that her mother had phoned to say she was staying the night in Carlisle. She then rang the restaurant and booked a table for two.

Robert returned, looking spruce and fresh, in a clean shirt and newly-pressed slacks. Anne allowed her eyes to flicker over him with affection. As though aware of her regard, he squeezed her hand as they went to the car.

"Thank you very much for the day," she said formally, as they were driving along. "I feel so much better now. All my hysterics have gone. You've cut everything down to size."

"My pleasure," he said, and patted her on the knee.

There was a car parked outside Lowater and a man stood waiting in the porch. Both Robert and Anne recognised car and man at the same time. James Millard was the man and the car was his beautiful luxurious model she had once driven.

Maureen had gone and the house was locked up. "I wonder how long he's been there," Anne said.

"I'm sorry to barge in on you like this," James said when they had greeted one another. "I suppose I should have phoned."

"Mother's away for the night," Anne said, and when James looked rather downcast she said, "But she's only an hour or so away, in Carlisle. Shall I phone her and tell her you're here?"

"Could you? Would you?" he said with a certain desperation.

Anne unlocked the front door. "Come in. You look as if you could do with a drink."

"I'm afraid I'm also the bearer of bad news," James said a little wearily. "Natalie has run off with your fiancé, Jack Cooper."

Anne turned from the drinks table where

she was pouring out a drink for him. "What did you say?"

"I'm sorry to be the one to tell you." He fumbled at an inside pocket and brought out a folded sheet of writing-paper. "This is the letter she left me this morning." He gave it to Robert and after reading it, Robert silently handed it to Anne.

"*Darling Pa,*" the letter ran, in Natalie's round, childish handwriting, "*I am sorry to do this to you but it seemed the best way—at least to avoid all sorts of scenes. I am in love with Jack Cooper and we are going to get married. Maybe, when you read this, I might already be married, by special licence. I knew you would not approve of this but I am sure you will when you see how happy I am. You cannot deny me my happiness when you are so sure your own is with Barbara. Jack and I have bought a simply beautiful caravan, our home-on-wheels, and we plan to go abroad as soon as possible. Please do not worry about me, darling. I am quite old enough to know what I am doing and we are going to exciting life. Jack and I have been in love ever since we first met. I am sorry for Anne but she never really understood him. He has been trying to break it off with her for ages but she wouldn't*

318

let him, and I think his kind heart didn't want to hurt her too much. I will write again as soon as I can and tell you where I am. Expect to get all sorts of cards from all sorts of fabulous places! Natalie."

"I am afraid this is very hard for you," James said.

"I'm all right," Anne said quickly. She felt Robert put a comforting hand on her shoulder. "Please," she said, "I am quite all right. Jack and I had broken things off."

"You don't have to be brave," said Robert.

"I am not being brave," said Anne a little wildly. She turned to James. "What are you going to do? You can't let Natalie marry that man." She remembered Jack's words—"You're not the only string to my bow." Natalie had been his ace in the hole.

"Has Natalie money of her own?" she asked James.

"Yes, I'm afraid she has. She is completely independent. She inherited all her mother's money and besides, I have settled a fair amount on her . . . She's emptied her desk—credit cards, cheque-book, passport are all gone . . ."

Natalie had bought Ermentrude. Natalie

was going to finance the trip round the world.

"But how can we stop them?" asked Robert. "Natalie is of age, and independent. Do you know where they would go, Anne?"

"I have no idea," said Anne slowly, "but I know someone who might. I'll ring up the Brackens."

Robert looked at her, a sad expression in his eyes. "The end of a perfect day," he said. "Are you sure you're all right, Anne? Even if you stop them getting married or running off together, it doesn't mean Jack will come back to you."

Anne put her hands on top of her head. "Do you know what I would like to do?" she asked. "Lie on the floor and beat my heels and scream! *I do not care what happens to Jack*! I mind what happens to Natalie. She must not get involved with him."

"I also mind what happens to Natalie," said Robert. "Let's try and find out where they might have gone."

16

SOME hours later, Anne sat in an easy-chair sipping a long, soothing drink of tea. She was sitting in the darkness and she was alone. The end of a perfect day.

She had phoned her mother. She had phoned the Brackens. The Brackens had come up with two addresses which might lead to Jack: his flat and his wife's flat. Robert had driven off to London forthwith. He would stay the night there—with his parents or in his own place.

Barbara Tyson had driven from Carlisle and had arrived some two hours later. She and James were now sitting at the restaurant table which Anne had reserved for herself and Robert and having, she hoped, a delicious reconciliation. For that, it was clear, was what James had come about. He was upset and distressed about his daughter and he wanted Barbara's love and comfort in his dilemma.

And Robert? He had gone to rescue

Natalie as willingly as any knight errant. Anne sighed. It had been a blissful day. She allowed herself the pleasure of thinking about Robert—his voice, his eyes, the whole sum of him. She loved him. She had learnt a lot about him—not, perhaps, his size in socks, but he did like garlic. He had become both more approachable and more mysterious.

She loved him. Did he feel anything for her other than that she was kissable? Perhaps she would never know. Perhaps it was Natalie he carried a torch for. And yet, and yet—She didn't want a bit of Robert. She wanted all of him like any other corny, love-sick maiden. To try and comfort herself, Anne went and put on some records, and then went to bed.

The next morning, James and Barbara told her they had had a wonderful evening. It was obvious from their pleased and happy faces they were reconciled. Robert had phoned and said so far he had drawn a blank, but Jack's ex-wife seemed to think she might be hearing from him soon as he had apparently written to her about the child some days previously.

"A child?" said James.

"He's been married before," Anne said.

"Oh, my dear!" her mother said.

"Mother, please don't start being sympathetic again. How often do I have to protest Jack means nothing to me? I was a fool. You were right. Surely that admission will convince you?" Anne repeated her words slowly and emphatically "*I was wrong. You were right.*"

"But you seem so distrait and unhappy," her mother said.

"Wouldn't you be distrait if you'd had a strike on your hands?"

James was going to stay at Lowater with her mother for a few days—or at least until they had news of Natalie—then they were going back to London and planning to be married immediately. "A registry office, I'm afraid," said her mother happily, "but we'll have a blessing in a church somewhere afterwards, probably up here, and we're going to have a party in London, and another in Grayham for our friends, and one up here—a grand celebration."

"And Natalie? What of Natalie?"

"I hope she'll be here—and if she's not, we'll have to be ready to pick up the pieces

—in a week, a month or a year. It can't last."

But they had, in the end, to be ready sooner than that. Robert arrived back with Natalie on the following day, Sunday. Robert had not told them he was coming back with her, and they arrived unexpectedly about noon.

Barbara and James and Anne heard the car and came outside to see who it was.

Natalie jumped out of the car, as gay as a bird, and ran straight into her father's arms. Barbara followed father and daughter into the house.

Robert looked at Anne and raised his eyes to heaven. It had apparently not been difficult to trace Natalie. She herself, when she heard that Robert was looking for her, came to his flat of her own accord and told him she was ready to come home. She had discovered that Jack had no intention of marrying her and Natalie, apparently, was old-fashioned enough to want to be married. The romantic, travelling, gypsy life included marriage as far as she was concerned.

"We didn't expect you so soon," Anne said.

"I wasn't going to hang round London any longer than I could help. I'm afraid Natalie was not too pleased at having to get up so early. She seemed to think my rescue mission included a holiday jaunt round town."

"She doesn't seem very upset," ventured Anne.

Robert shrugged. "We were having the traumas, not her; I think it was all rather a lark to her," he said, "But the whole episode has certainly made her father see sense. Natalie has her own life to lead and she's going her own way, and he now knows that—and that he must think of his own and Barbara's happiness . . ." He clapped his hands together in a kind of brushing motion. "But that's enough of Natalie." He looked at her, his face set in tense, grim lines. "Why didn't you tell me you had broken off with Jack?"

"I didn't think you'd be that interested."

"That's codswallop. I've made my interest in you pretty plain all these weeks."

"You were interested just as much in other people—more. Margot . . ."

"Margot! Margot was a gadfly—a

distraction. She stopped me thinking of you night and day . . . Dare I think you were jealous of Margot? Friday—that beautiful day on the water—you could have told me so easily you had finished with Jack . . . and there I was suffering, because I thought you'd had a lovers' quarrel, and choosing to be noble and not making love to you, trying to comfort you because you were unhappy . . . thinking I'd have to bide my time and be patient and cunning . . ."

"If you had been perspicacious, you'd have seen I wore no ring . . ."

"I'm not very clever about signs like that," he said softly. "Besides, I thought you'd quarrelled and you were terribly unhappy about it . . . so unhappy that you didn't want to talk about it . . ."

"I wanted to tell you," said Anne. She looked away from him, unable to meet his eyes. "You were so kind, but I felt it would be like laying myself on a plate, saying, 'See, I'm free, I'm available '—and you might not have wanted to take advantage of the invitation . . . and that I could not have borne . . ."

"And are you available?" he asked huskily. "Oh, Anne, look at me. Tell me I needn't sigh over you any more, that I needn't spend any more sleepless nights thinking of you . . ." He took a step towards her and pulled her into his arms. "I love you, Anne darling. I think I loved you the moment I set eyes on you wearing that blue overall, do you remember? But it took me a while before I realised how much . . . and you were so cold and un-approachable, so self-contained, and in love with that creature Jack . . . and all my overtures you ignored or rejected . . ."

He kissed her long and lingeringly. When she came up for air, Anne said, "We can't stay here—in the middle of the drive —it's so public . . ."

"I shouldn't think anyone is looking out of the window at us," said Robert still holding her. "They've got plenty of other things to occupy them."

He stroked her hair back from her face. "Why don't we go for a walk? You've never shown me the tarn . . ."

So they walked up into the fells behind the house and found the lonely little tarn, clear and bright as a jewel, reflecting the blue sky in its cold, crystal depths; and there, sitting among the curling green fronds of the newly-sprouting bracken, they plighted their troth, swore to be true to each other, and promised they would be happy together for ever and ever.

THE END